HAMMER OF GOD

THE MISADVENTURES OF LOREN BOOK 3

INES JOHNSON

THOSE JOHNSON GIRLS

1

"What do you mean I can't go?"

The E string of violins envied the high-pitched note that my shrill voice reached. Men hated that sound, especially when it came out of a woman during an argument. It went straight to the recesses of their reptile brains where their tiny reserves of emotion were stored. Hit the right hysterical note and it could drive them to spontaneously combust on the spot.

My body vibrated like a master player pulling those angsty notes from an instrument. Arthur, leader of the Knights of the Roundtable and my boss as I was the latest person to be knighted, scratched at his massive chest. His ragged nail snagged in the linen of his loose tunic. The tunic dipped open, revealing an eyeful of the dusting of hairs on his defined chest.

I had no interest in Arthur's defined chest or the muscled pecs or that perfectly formed valley that would nicely fit a woman's head for cuddling after sex. Crazy how a guy being your boss and restricting your movements and acting like he was your father could turn your sex drive cold.

"Loren, you're telling me you want to go to another realm and steal the hammer of a god so that you can go down into the core of the earth and rescue your friend."

"Best friend," I corrected.

"Oh. My mistake." Arthur held up his hands in acquiescence.

Good, I was buttering him up. With a bit more badgering, he'd be toast. Strongest knight in Camelot he might be, but at the end of the day, he was still a man.

Men were weak when it came to arguing with women. They built up their physical muscle for hand to hand battles, but they were feeble when it came to emotional warfare. Their lack of emotional training left the male species easily outwitted and outmatched during arguments where feelings trumped logic.

"The answer is still no," said Arthur.

My jaw tensed. My fingers curled into fists. I knew better than to reach for my sword against him.

I still had plenty in my emotional arsenal. High-pitched hysteria wasn't working. But there was still hand wringing, the lip tremble, the doe eyes. Or I could go straight for the big guns; tears.

Looking at Arthur, I figured I still had some room before the heavy arsenal was needed. I decided to keep using my words but go at him from various angles. A blitz offensive starting with pointing out his patterns of unfair behavior toward me.

"You're constantly holding me back."

Arthur opened his mouth, but I couldn't let him respond. I had to keep him off balance and distract him with things he hadn't done yet.

"You'd let another knight go if he asked. *He* probably wouldn't even need to ask."

I could see Arthur's mind trying to process that quick turn of blame. To keep him unsteady and lopsided, I hit him with a present issue.

"Need I remind you that you saved your own

brother, even after Merlin caused the death of people in this community? All Nia's ever done is help."

And to complete the circle of offense, I hit him with a far-fetched idea that should send him reeling.

"You know what I think? I think you're afraid to let me go because when I get to this other realm they'll recognize me for my true worth and want to keep me."

Arthur's head waggled as though he were considering this angle.

Uh oh. So that last attack might've been a mistake. Maybe it was time to bring out the big guns after all. Problem was, I'd never been a crier.

I had been an only child. My parents had given me all of their attention from the moment I was born until the moment they each passed away. During that glorious time with them, I typically got my way.

Not that I was spoiled. More because I was the only one ever asking for anything, being the only grabby-handed kid. And I didn't ask for outrageous things. Normally.

But the hell if I was done in present day, face to face with my new keeper. "You're not the boss of me."

"Actually," said Arthur, "I am. You took vows remember."

"Of chivalry, not marriage." See, this is why I didn't believe in marriage. I could barely stomach long-term commitments.

What now? I couldn't flirt with Arthur. Or run him through with a sword. What did a woman do with a man she couldn't seduce or kill or emotionally manipulate?

"It's too dangerous," Arthur continued.

"What? Because I'm a woman? Morgan's right. Your misogyny is showing."

"The quest you're proposing is both blasphemous and suicidal."

"You would go," I said. "You would pick up your sword and ride out in a blaze of glory if it were for anyone in this town."

"It's not for someone in this town. It's Nia. She's immortal. She can take care of herself."

"You heard Igraine. She's being held. She can't escape. How many times has she come to your aide?"

"You mean when she wasn't stealing from me?"

Details, details. Truth was the enemy of any argument. But I'd play it his way for now. "Nia saved the Grail. She saved Gwin. She's saved me. She's my family."

I'd never been that girl who had girlfriends. I got along better with guys. The problem was, I wasn't sleeping with any of these knights. And I no longer had the inclination to. They were all my brothers.

"The best thing to do is to let Mohandis handle this."

Tresor Mohandis stood off to the side, quiet and still like the mountain of a man he was. He leaned one of his broad shoulders against the wall. It chafed that he was witnessing me being effectively grounded by Arthur.

"We'll help you get to the other realm." Arthur addressed Tres directly, talking over my head. "But we can't cross there. We have a treaty with Odin."

Odin? The Norse god of creation?

My dad was Dutch, yet his German roots seemed to interest him the least. But still, I knew about the Asgardians; Odin, Thor, Freya.

Igraine had said we needed the Hammer of God to save Nia. The Norse god running around twirling a hammer was Thor. Somewhere in another realm, there was a real-life Hemsworth running around flinging thunderbolts and no one had told me!

"You know how to get there?" asked Tres.

It was the first sound Tres had muttered since coming inside and telling me that Nia and Zane were dead. He had believed them to be dead, until we went into the kitchen and Igraine set us straight.

Nia and Zane had fallen into a crack in the earth. But instead of dying like normal human beings, they'd simply gone back to the place of their birth, because they weren't normal human beings. They were Immortal, and at the moment, they were grounded by their parents until further notice. So, of course, I was going to bust my bestie and her boyfriend out.

Tres's eyes had been so downcast when he'd come into the castle earlier to deliver the news. There was a glimmer of hope in his eyes now. But his face was mostly shuttered, holding his emotions close to his chest.

Tres loved Nia. He'd risked his life for her more than once already. Just once, I wish someone would come after me without a care for their own life and limb.

Arthur was currently sizing up Tres. The two had a history as complicated as his history with Nia. But it looked like Tres passed muster. The valiant knight beckoned the dark immortal out of the room and left me standing there.

My gaze went doe wide with indignation. Angry

tears pricked the corners of my eyes. I'd just been cockblocked.

I wasn't going to take this lying down. Regardless of what anyone might've said, I wasn't that kind of woman, and this argument wasn't over. I stormed off after the men.

2

I followed Tres and Arthur out of the kitchen. Both men were large and ate up the distance with their wide gaits. Marching double time, I caught up as they passed the Great Hall.

There, the townsfolk's merriment rose to my ears. It was after dinner, but a few people still lingered. Every man's head inclined with respect as Arthur passed by. Many women looked up beneath hooded gazes or batted their eyelashes outright at Tres.

I assumed Arthur was headed for the Throne Room where the Round Table sat to conduct this business. But no. We continued on down the winding stairwell. Here, I moved easily with my slight frame. Both Arthur and Tres had to turn their bodies slightly to the side to fit.

At the bottom of the stairs, I turned my body to go into the weapons room, figuring Arthur might feel this discussion would best be had with heavy artillery within reach. But, no. We passed that room too.

I spied Yuric and Maurice inside on cleaning duty. Baysle jumped to his feet from behind the gaming console and dropped the controller when he saw Arthur. Arthur's attention was focused farther down the hall and the little weasel's fecklessness wasn't caught. But I pointed at my eyes with my middle and index finger, then pointed at him with only my middle finger to let him know I was watching him.

My buddies, Yuric and Maurice, gave me questioning glances. But I could only shrug to indicate I had no idea where I was headed. Because I didn't.

I didn't even know there were more rooms beyond this hall, and I had snooped in every nook and cranny in this old castle. Or, so I thought.

Arthur, Tres, and I headed past the dungeons and down an even lower layer. At one point, when we walked past the rust bars of a cell with there was the taste of iron in the air wafting off broken manacles, Tres turned to me. His expression was easy to read.

Am I walking into a trap? His face said.

The hell if I know, I shrugged. *It'd be you and me both.*

Finally, we reached a simple wooden door. Only there was no latch on the doorpost. Arthur gave a distinctive, complicated, Morse code of a knock on the undecorated wood. From the other side, I heard locks and bolts rattling and unfastening. The door was thrown back to reveal Percy.

Sir Percivale was bare-chested. Low slung leather pants rested on his narrow hips. His feet were bare. His light eyes flitted about in his head like they scanned everything on the surface of the scene and then slipped past another layer to take a deeper look.

All the while, his eyelids jumped and jerked as he held his stare. His molars ground behind his pursed lips. His fists balled and flexed, knuckles cracking with each clench.

I knew without anyone having to warn me that Percy was cray-cray. He leaned against the jamb of the doorframe with one arm over his head. His thick bicep blocked any view inside the room.

I was momentarily fixed on the long hairs in his armpit. He'd taken a moment to braid them. Weird.

There was a hum of activity coming from within the four walls of the room. Like a horde of bees, gnats, wasps and any other tiny insect that swarmed around a large mammal's head.

"Yeah, boss?" Percy asked. His voice barreled unwillingly from his chest like a boulder hefted up with great force only to roll crashing down the side once it was shoved free.

"I need a word," said Arthur.

Percy glanced over Arthur's shoulder. He didn't bother me with his scrutinizing. I wasn't sure whether to take that as a compliment that he trusted me, or as an insult that he didn't see me as a threat.

It was Tres that the knight's eyes landed on. Percy and Tres looked as though they could be cousins. Both men had the sandy, golden brown skin of the desert. Their jaws were the harsh angles of sand dunes. Their brows arched like the top of a sheik's tent. Only their eye color was different.

Percy's were bright, sharp as glass. Tres's were dark but there was a lightness in the center. Sharp met light. They did that silent exchange thing that men did. Twitching their eyes and flaring their nostrils and puffing up their chests. The dialogue to the scene probably went something like this:

I can totally kick your ass with one hand tied behind my back.

Oh yeah? I can do it with both hands tied and a bum knee.

Well, I bagged more booty than you.

I'm massively endowed and don't need to count my bounty.

Arthur cleared his throat and the staring contest ended. Before I knew it, Tres and Percy shook their respective bits of equipment and the pissing contest was over. Percy backed up and opened the door wide.

With his body no longer obstructing the view, I gaped at what I saw inside. Arthur and Tres were already inside, but my footsteps slowed as I walked into what could only be called a war room.

There were screens everywhere. Receivers showing green blips. Monitors displaying lines of code. Video feeds broadcasting open areas and densely populated streets. And ... was that a live shot of Westminster Abbey? And over there on that other screen, was that an interior of the White House's Situation Room?

Honestly, that's not what had me gasping out loud.

Percy had arranged himself in a chair surrounded by another set of wide television screens. There was rugby on one, American football on another, and WWE wrestling on a third. If I didn't know him any better (and I'm not sure I did) I might question which side he played on. No European watched guys in tights crashing into each other chasing after a pigskin. Every man worth anything knew that balls belonged on the floor and were only handled with feet.

The NFL? Really, Percy?

A tumbler of hard whiskey sat on a side table. I'd stopped worrying about Percy's liver the second week of knowing him. He was never sloshed. He had no tolerance for drunkenness. Whiskey was like Kool-Aid for him.

After quests, Percy always disappeared. I figured he preferred to unwind alone. I supposed that process took place in his room with the violence and whiskey. Once he'd gathered his wits after his self-imposed solitude, he'd emerge and was his normal loud and boisterous self.

But I see now that, as loud as he was, he was an

introvert at heart. Sir Percivale got recharged by solitude and quiet, watching violent visuals and downing strong spirits. I wondered if we had a psychologist in the village? Might be a good idea if we didn't want Camelot to end up like Waco one day.

"We have a situation," said Arthur once the door was closed.

"What do you need?" asked Percy. "A code cracked? Someone tracked down? A body buried?"

"Entry into the fae realm," said Arthur.

That called Percy up short. His left hand shook, but the shaking appeared beyond his control. I'd never seen the knight rattled.

The wildness in Percy's eyes magnified with each word that left his lips. "I'm not going back to Alfheim."

Alfheim? Why did it sound familiar? Was that what the fae realm was called.

"You've been to the fae realm?" I asked. "No one tells me anything."

"We don't need you to go back," Arthur said. "Just help Mohandis get in."

Percy turned his wild gaze to Tres. "Wow, you're still pissed at him for Evangeline?"

About two hundred years ago, Tres had trifled with a witch. I'd met the woman. Evangeline was five hundred years old and looked to be in her late forties or maybe early fifties by human standards. She was happy about the trifle of an affair and would talk anyone's ear off about her escapade with Tres. Yeah, I'd listened to her, more than once. But knights didn't countenance anybody messing with their witches without putting a ring on it.

"They'll eat him alive," Percy was saying.

"Who?" I asked. "Fairies?"

I could believe it. I'd met the fair kind. They were as beautiful as described in children's books. But they were also bloodthirsty, conniving miscreants.

"Not the fae," said Percy. "The Valkyrie."

"Valkyrie?" I asked.

I was starting to put two and five together. Alfheim, Valkyrie. These were all Norse mythology. Valkyrie were women in armor who chose fallen mortal soldiers and carried their souls to Valhalla. They were the Norse representation of Amazonians, like German Wonder Women.

"They're real?" The adolescent girl inside me squealed with delight.

But Percy ignored me and kept his focus on Tres.

"A big, strong man like you? They'll take one look at you and cart you off to Valhalla."

"What's a Valkyrie?" Tres asked.

I raised my hand, ready with my know-it-all answer. They all ignored me.

"You know what a siren is?" Percy asked. "Beautiful women in the water that lure men to their deaths. Those fools are happy to go when they hear the women's seductive songs."

What did sirens have to do with Valkyrie? Percy was getting his lore mixed up. Sirens were Greek.

"Valkyrie don't sing, and their beauty would make a siren look like a troll," Percy continued. "They don't get in the water, though the seas would probably part for them before a drop would dare muss their hair or mar their boots. They fly on dragons and wield swords forged in light. They lead the souls of the dead to Valhalla to their father, Odin. But they have a taste for men."

"Carnal?" I asked.

"Carnivorous," said Percy.

I was failing to see how this Valhalla wasn't a fool's paradise for men. I suspected there was a line queued up outside the walls.

"They'll strip your flesh and eat your soul," said Percy. "At least that's what the fae told their sprouts."

"I'm told the Hammer of God is in this realm," said Tres.

"Odin's hammer?" asked Percy.

"I thought it was Thor's Hammer?" I said.

"There are many hammers," said Percy. "What do you want to do with the hammer you're questing after?"

"We need to travel to the core of the earth," said Tres.

"You want to travel between the realms?" asked Percy. "Then it's Odin's hammer you want. It allows him to take the souls between the nine realms. He won't part with it. And you won't be able to get past his daughters to even get to him. Not with your flesh intact. A big, strong warrior like you? The Valkyrie will eat your soul."

"We need that hammer to rescue Nia," I said.

"Oh? You sure that tight piece of ass is worth it?"

Tres bristled. That soft spot in his eyes turned hard. His knuckles cracked as his fists balled.

"Yeah," I glared at Percy. "She is."

"Do you know a way in or not?" said Tres through gritted teeth.

"I know a way out," said Percy.

If the stories were correct, and I'd learned all of the Arthurian tales held a kernel of truth, Percy was raised in the wild with his mother. What if that wild was the fae realm?

"If you got out, then there must be a way in," I said.

Percy sighed, but then he coughed it up. "The Bermuda Triangle."

3

"Please let me know if there's anything more I can do for you, Mr. Mohandis." Gwin had her hands folded primly in front of her. Ever the consummate hostess, her smile was everything accommodating and proper as she stood before the room that had been made up for Tres's overnight stay.

Behind me, I heard the low rumble of a growl. Lance's ginger head was bowed, but I could've sworn I saw sparks fly as he turned on his heel and stalked down the hall.

Gwin frowned in confusion and concern as she looked down the hall after Lance's retreating figure. Tres arched a knowing eyebrow at the knight's back. When he turned back to Gwin, his smile held not an ounce of propriety. He looked grateful, and a touch humble, at her show of hospitality.

"I'm sure my brief stay will rival that of any five-star hotel." Tres's deep voice was silky smooth as it rolled off his tongue.

Gwin smiled, visibly unaffected by the sensuality that positively oozed out of the man's pores without him even trying. I knew my cousin preened over the comparison to the five stars of hospitality.

Lance had nothing to worry about on either front. Tres wasn't trying to woo Gwin. I'd seen him try with Nia. He'd easily befuddled my practical, pragmatic, perpetually poised friend. If Tres wanted Gwin, he could probably persuade her, or at least turn her head for a few days.

But Gwin's interests lay elsewhere. The repository of her affection was retreating down the hall in an angry huff of red hair.

Beside me, Morgan shivered as she inhaled, likely catching a whiff of that musky scent that seemed to cling to Tresor Mohandis's skin. Frankincense was it? The essential oil had always reminded me of religious ceremonies and cleansing rituals. But when it mixed with Tres's skin, it took on a sensuous note.

"Unlike a hotel," growled Arthur, "we don't offer

any turndown service, or room service, or any other *services* you might be used to."

"I can bring you up a plate of dinner," said Morgan. "You're probably famished from your journey here."

Arthur sent the dark-haired woman a glare, which she didn't even notice. Even if she had, it wasn't as if that would cow Morgan.

"Thank you everyone, for your ... hospitality," said Tres. "I'm simply going to turn down the sheets myself, climb in them alone, and rest before heading out in the morning on the next leg of my journey."

Gwin looked at Tres with empathy. Morgan regarded him with disappointment. Arthur glared at him with suspicion.

"That's a good idea," I said. "Get a good night's rest and then we'll get an early start for Bermuda in the morning."

Arthur whirled on me. "We discussed this."

"*We* actually didn't," I said. "*You* gave a command."

"Because I'm your leader. You are supposed to follow my commands."

"I thought we were equals. Isn't that why we sit at a round table and not a square one or a triangular one? Or even one of those trapezoid ones you see in school rooms."

"That's enough, Loren."

The gust of hot air from his words brushed across my heated cheeks. The fine hairs on my forearms and neck stood at attention. All ten of my fingers twitched, along with my eyes. Warning lights flashed in my brain. The lights formed the words fight or flight.

If I were a better person, I'd see the dark circles under Arthur's eyes and know that he'd been under a great deal of stress these last few months; the Grail, Templars, Banduri, assaults, deaths, invasion, family drama. I'm certain having me tossed into his lap wasn't making things any easier.

But I didn't give a crap about any of that right now. My best friend was in danger. And Arthur had just yelled at me in front of freakin' Tresor Mohandis.

Instead of compassion, like my cousin Gwin would show, and instead of defiance, like my cousin Morgan would show, I balled my hands into fists.

I lowered my gaze. I took a step back in retreat. The big brute bought it, 'cause he let go of his glare on me and turned it to Tres.

"There are guards posted at every corner," said

Arthur. "We take security very seriously inside the castle. So, you will be safe while you remain inside those particular four walls." Arthur's hands indicated the bedroom behind Tres, which resided on a deserted floor of the castle, that was easy access to the dungeons.

"Again," said Tres, "your hospitality knows no bounds."

"As long as you mind the boundaries."

Tres nodded. Then he ducked into the room and closed the door. To add injury to Arthur's insults, there was the sound of the lock clicking into place to bar anyone's entrance.

Arthur turned to the three of us. When he realized he was faced with the three Galahad girls, he moaned. Then he made a shooing motion with his hands.

"Out," he barked. "The lot of you. I don't want any of you on this floor."

"But what if the poor man needs something in the night?" said Gwin.

I knew for a fact that, salacious though they may sound, Gwin meant those words solely and purely in her role as the Lady of the Castle. It was a role that remained hers as the long-suffering wife of the eldest Pendragon male. Merlin, the murderous bastard, still rested in the infirmary, still waiting patiently to die.

When Morgan spoke, it was in no way hospitable. It was purely lustful. "Yeah, he might need a new pillow. But one that's made of warm flesh and blood instead of feathers."

"Out!" Arthur's roar was loud enough to shake a few of the stones from the castle walls.

Not a single one of us jumped. A man putting a little bass in his voice only worked on those who feared assault. Every witch knew that there wasn't a knight alive who would lay a feather on her in violence.

We did hurry out of the hall though. Arthur might not raise a finger to us, but he could make our lives difficult if we pushed him far enough. By the look on his face, he was standing at the edge of his patience.

The three of us opted for self-preservation. Gwin headed to the kitchens. Morgan headed to the library. I headed to the stables. I figured I might as well get in a ride before I snuck out tomorrow for my trip to Bermuda.

I was headed out to sea again. This time purposefully trying to get snared in the aquatic net of the Bermuda Triangle. I needed a better travel agent.

Nia and I had set sail in the Mediterranean Sea last year. We'd met rough seas on our journey. I'd quickly lost the contents of my stomach, came close to losing my life, but my bestie had blocked Death's door.

It wasn't the first time she'd saved my ass. I'd saved hers more than once. It was like that between us. Looked like that pattern was about to be repeated. I was determined it would be repeated for decades to come.

There was no way I wasn't going after her. Nia was the only person who loved me in spite of my faults. Well, that wasn't true. My family in Camelot —Gwin, Morgan, Igraine, and increasingly more of the knights—were coming to do the same. But Nia was the first since my parents had died. She was the first of my chosen family, and if she was trapped in hell, then I was going down there too.

The back door closed behind me with a snick as fresh air greeted me. The air was warm with heat that could only come from a large mass of hotness. I wasn't alone. A tall drink of water that had blended in with the night showed itself.

"You got out?" I said.

Tres lifted an arched eyebrow, as though to say *duh*. He looked like a chieftain standing in the moonlight, what of the moonlight I could see. His broad shoulders nearly blocked the orb from sight. I wondered if I'd have to start spinning a thousand and one tales in order to escape his clutches.

"Problem with our hospitality?" I asked.

Tres snorted. But coming from him it sounded like a bull raring to charge. "It's as I would expect."

"Well, you did break the first rule of knight club; don't tussle with their witches."

"It was the witch in question that did the tussling. I was just along for the ride."

I moved into the darkness, closer to him. Lulled there by that earthy scent of him. I wondered if this was exactly how Evangeline had been snared by this thief of the night. But Tres's hands were behind his back. They weren't reaching out to muss even my hair.

"What are you doing out here?" I asked. "Taking off early?"

"Room's a little smaller than I'm used to."

I didn't take the insult to Camelot's accommodations personally. I didn't believe him. I'd camped with this man before out in the middle of nowhere. The size of the room wasn't what plagued him.

Tres had explained that before Nia and Zane had fallen to their apparent deaths, they'd all been below ground, beneath a serpent mound on Native American land. They'd been looking for a way into a mystical world where they believed they came from, and they'd found it. But it had swallowed up Nia and Zane whole.

"I've been in close quarters for longer than I'd like," Tres continued. His eyes were haunted with what had to be memories of seeing both the woman he loved and his own best friend slip through his fingers. "I just needed the fresh air."

"She's going to be fine," I said coming closer to him. "We're going to get her back."

"I never expected to win her," he said. "She never looked at me the way she looked at him."

Him was Zane. Nia's on again, off again lover. They had been off for the last couple of months, and Tres had moved in. But with a grand gesture of dying alongside her, I supposed Zane had the advantage now.

I really liked Zane. His artistic, bohemian soul called to mine. We got along famously. But I'd been rooting for Tres. The dude was rich, and I only wanted the best for my friend.

And, yeah, maybe to tag along on shopping

sprees and fancy vacations funded by the billionaire. But in my heart, I knew that it would always come back to Nia being with Zane. Inevitability was written all over those two.

"Nia and Zane, they have *a thing*," I said.

"What *thing*?" asked Tres.

"You know, that *thing*. That silent, wordless thing that is so loud it precedes them when they enter a room. That thing that when you stand next to them, it's like you're standing at the center of an electric grid and it raises the goosebumps on your skin. That thing where if you walk in the middle of them gazing at each other, it makes your heart skip a beat. That thing where you never truly have all of their attention if they're looking dead at you because you know they're still thinking about the other one. That thing where they even start to look like one another."

"Yeah," sighed Tres. "That *thing*."

We stood in silence for a moment. My words might have been cruel to a guy who wanted to have a thing with the woman in that example. But my words were also honest.

"I've always wanted a thing," I said. "But I've come to the realization that I'm not that kind of girl who gets things. I mean, I get my share of things if you know what I mean."

Tres's expression told me he knew what I meant. Then he closed his eyes as though it were just too much to see the world, even in the darkness.

"I've just never gotten to have my own thing. Wait. You know what I mean when I'm saying *thing* this time?"

"Yeah." He didn't open his eyes. "I've never had my own *thing* either."

Tres turned his face up into the moonlight. Like Arthur, he had bags under his eyes. I could see the weight of the world settling down on his broad shoulders. He looked so alone. Standing next to him and the heat coming off his big body, I shivered. Damn. We were the saddest sacks of saps.

"I'm not a good guy," he said.

"I'm not a good girl." I swear I wasn't hitting on him. With me, words just came out dirty naturally.

"I've been in a lot of stories," he said. "Myths, legends, fairytales. I don't understand how I continually get cast as the villain who never gets the girl?"

He looked truly befuddled.

"You're not a bad guy," I said.

"Would you tell that to the scribes and the poets and whatever gods made up the idea of fate?"

"You don't believe in fate?"

"No, I don't. I'm going to go up against a god, risk

my life, rescue the girl, and she'll still choose another guy. Still, the ending of the story won't change for me."

I couldn't argue that; the bit about Nia choosing Zane. But I could alter his story a bit. "Maybe we won't get the romance, but we can be heroes."

"Arthur said you can't go."

I smirked.

Tres let out a laugh for the first time since he'd arrived.

"The romance story ends with the happily ever after," I said. "But, in the hero's story, the hero lives on to continue the fight. Let's be heroes."

A slow grin spread across his face. "I leave at dawn. I have a yacht docked in Cardiff."

"I'll meet you there," I said. "Not a moment too late. Wouldn't want you to turn into a pumpkin."

"Wouldn't that happen at midnight?" he asked.

"Yes, but—"

"And it's a yacht, not a coach."

"Would you just hush and allow me my metaphors."

4

It took me a long time to get over the death of my dad. Not to say that getting over my mother's death was any easier. But I had spent all of my life with my dad by the time of his death and less than half with my mom.

He was the only man that's ever truly loved me. A father's love is an amazing thing. A father looks at his daughter like she's made of stardust. He treats her just as precious as if she's fallen from the heavens.

Well, the good ones do. And I'd had a good one. I'd had the best one.

I believed the only love that was real between a woman and a man would be with a dad; real, true, unconditional love that asked for nothing in return.

So imagine my surprise when the first person who loved me after my dad died was a woman.

Nia's and my journey to BFFs began in the same fashion of most women's friendships. I manipulated her into doing me a favor. What? Is that not how girlfriends normally connect?

After Nia and I set off on our maiden adventure, with her trying to ditch me and me cyberstalking her whereabouts until I found her ...

Is that wrong too?

Oh. I see it now. Crazy ex-girlfriend move. Now I see why she was mad.

I also didn't tell Nia the whole truth of why I needed her help. Lies weren't black and white to me —that was racist. There were full lies, and little lies, and half-truths, and cones of silence.

I'd have told a full lie to get Nia's help to clear my dad's name if it was necessary. But I didn't have to. I gave Nia half-truths which were my first hint that we'd be true friends. And eventually, she did learn the full truth.

Yeah, I may have been forced to tell the truth when our lives were placed in peril. When we were bound with blades pointed at our throats, I came totally clean with her, which strengthened the bond between us. Eventually.

My dad had been a world-renowned archaeologist. He'd been very sought after by the intellectuals of the world. He was called in to consult on the Parthenon restoration in Greece. We were always stopping off in the Valley of the Kings in Egypt to offer insight. We'd also spent a lot of time in the Sterkfontein Caves of South Africa where the largest number of hominid fossils were unearthed.

I'd had an amazing childhood filled with adventure and discovery. I was extended the respect that was bestowed upon my father. I was indulged. Until it went away.

One day in the Gongyi province of Southern China, my dad had come across something he couldn't explain; a dragon bone. Not from a flying lizard. Dragon bones were the bones of ox and turtles used by the ancient Chinese before parchment was invented. The bones were common, but this particular bone told a secret. An ancient society, thought nearly extinct, had killed to protect it.

With a brush of his tools, my father only uncovered a layer of their secret. But it was enough. They didn't kill him. They did something far worse. They led him tumbling down the path to his ruination.

The Lin Kuei of the Gongyi didn't let my dad leave with the bone he'd found. So, my dad had forged one. His deception was found out, and he was made into a pariah in the world that had held him so high. His shame inevitably killed him.

Even worse, it killed him without him ever learning the truth of the bones.

Years later, Nia had unraveled it all. She solved the mystery, saved the day, got the boy, made a friend for life, and exonerated my dad. She'd become my hero and an unbreakable bond formed.

Bones and boys. Isn't that the way most girls bonded? I suppose most sisterhoods don't have a body count. Though I bet the number of girlfriends with blood on their hands might be surprising.

After that epic adventure, Nia and I became besties in the normal way—bonding together over our love lives. There was Nia and her on again, off again relationship with Zane. Nia and her will they, or won't they affair with Tres. There was my anathema to relationships and dedication to a good time with the three-legged humans who would hop on the ride and leave in the morning after a good time.

I would've been with Nia right now. Somewhere in the bowels of hell being grounded by her deity parents and trying to figure a way to sneak out. Instead, she'd left me behind in the care of my family to heal from my near-death experience after we saved the Holy Grail.

Served her right that she got caught and was on punishment. That'll teach her to go on a dangerous quest without me next time. Because there would be a next time.

The adventures of Dr. Nia Rivers and Lady Loren Van Alst were not over. Far from it. I'd tell whole and half lies to find my way to her. I'd beg and steal to get her back. Even if it meant misleading and disappointing my new family. I was willing to do anything to get my bestie back above ground. I knew just the accessory to help me do it.

Back in my room after my run in with Tres, I pulled the Ring of Gyges out of my dresser drawer. I didn't need a more secretive hiding spot. No one came into my room and ransacked anything. Trust was traded freely in this community.

The ring granted invisibility or invincibility to the wearer. I wasn't sure which? I hadn't tried it on since the gaming fairy, Gyges, had slipped it into my hand.

I'd won the ring in his tournament of horrors. Something I didn't particularly want to think about ever again. I should've given the ring to Arthur the moment I came back. I'm still not sure why I held onto it. Maybe because I knew something like this would happen, and I'd need to use its power.

A knock at my door had me jerking both hands behind my back. Both fists closed, one around the ring, the other around empty air. Was I about to force the intruder to guess which hand the ring was in? I was more powerful than a street corner magician. I probably could make the ring disappear. Or at least levitate it to somewhere safe.

"Loren? You decent?"

"Is she ever?"

I grinned at the sound of the two, deep, male voices on the other side of the door. They didn't barge in. They waited for my answer, like two gentlemen.

I shoved the ring down into my back pocket. It was the last place any male in this castle would deign to look. Especially these two.

I went over and pulled open the door. Geraint and Gawain stood on my threshold. The two were best friends. Aside from Gwin and Morgan, these two had been my first friends on the grounds.

Gawain had easily wrapped around my finger. It took Geraint some time to warm up to me, but we were chummy now. The suspicious brow he turned on me was simply apart of his natural features.

Geraint's broad shoulders filled my doorway. Gerry's eyes took me in in a quick, efficient sweep. Then his gaze swept past me to look into the room. His pupils shifted, taking in each of the four corners of the room, searching for threats as well as a tactical advantage. Finding no threat, his head turned back to me, his gaze softening at the edges.

Gawain rested his back against the wall of the dimly lit hall. Entirely unconcerned about his peril or potential hazards. It wasn't that Wain was care-less. He just knew the time and date of his appoint-ment with death and no longer looked out for dangers against his person.

"Hey GG," I said as I stepped aside and welcomed them into my sanctuary. Wain bounced on the edge of my bed and lounged back on an elbow. If I weren't a witch, and he wasn't convinced he'd meet death soon, I'd so totally join him there.

Gerry took the plush chair next to my closet. Halfway down, he froze. Reaching out his thumb and index finger, he gingerly moved a camisole from the armrest before sitting. Then rose again when he realized he was sitting on a bra. I wasn't the most tidy person.

"We came to check on you," said Wain. "We heard about Dr. Rivers."

"I'm sure Nia will be fine," said Gerry. "Mohandis will find her and take care of everything."

"Yeah," I dragged out the two syllables, affecting being bummed.

"Sorry about Arthur," said Wain.

"Though ... " Gerry began, but then winced like the words on the tip of his tongue tasted bittersweet. "I can see his point."

The room was silent and still. Each male stopped breathing as they regarded me, likely waiting for me to explode. I held still. They looked at each other, unsure how to proceed.

Gerry charged onward. "You just came off a quest. You were dealt a major blow with Baros the Bastard and his betrayal."

I looked away. I did not want to talk about my ex. Not about my embarrassment over thinking he actually loved me. Not about his offering my life as sacrifice for his. Not about his fate when his plan backfired.

"You're a knight," said Gerry. "You're not Super Woman. You can't do it all."

"The Knights are giving Mohandis our full support," said Wain.

I perked up at that. "Arthur's sending someone with Tres?"

"No," said Gerry. "We can't break the treaty."

"What exactly is this treaty?" I asked.

They looked at each other again. Their shared look only made me miss Nia more. We had our own set of shared looks. Most were one-way communications where she non-verbally said that I needed to shut my piehole.

"Our kind has been to the other realm before," said Gerry. "We went uninvited and we took something of value."

"What did we take?" I asked.

"Power," said Gerry. "The story of the apple and Eve? There's a basis of truth to it. One of our human ancestors ate of the Tree of Knowledge and became the first witch."

"The gods of that realm were not happy," said Wain. "They banished us from ever returning to that realm. Though some of them still steal humans every now and then for their amusement."

"And the Valkyrie are able to take their picks of humanity's fallen warriors," said Gerry. "But only the male warriors."

"Sexist, much?" I said.

"They won't take one of the children of Eve," said Gerry. "That's what they call our kind."

"Did Percy come from there?" I said.

"He was born in Alfheim and escaped," said Wain. "Barely. If any of us goes there, we break the treaty, which would mean the other kind could return to this realm as well, thus placing all of our kind and humanity in danger."

Crap. The stakes just got high. But I was still going. I only needed to make sure I wasn't caught when I got there.

"I know you want to rescue Nia," said Gerry. "But Mohandis is capable."

"Come out with us tonight," said Wain. "We'll get you good and drunk. Hopefully, by the time you sober up in a couple of days, Mohandis will be back with Nia in tow."

Any other night I'd love to go hang with the guys. Not this time. I had some sneaking out to do. "You guys are awesome to offer, but I'd just bring you down. I'm going to be too busy texting Tres every minute waiting for word."

The two looked at each other, once again exchanging unspoken words. I'd gotten close enough to them to know some of their looks. This one was their *don't trust that smile* look.

"We'll stay with you," said Gerry.

"No," I said, maybe a little too hasty. "I'm going to

turn in. I just need some time to myself. Come check on me in the morning."

There were no more looks. They each gave me a hug. Well, Wain did. Gerry wasn't good with affection. He rubbed me awkwardly on my shoulder.

Guilt snicked in my heart as the door closed, but not enough to deter me from my plan.

5

———

I awoke the next morning to birds chirping outside my window. The sun's rays stole across my face, stealing a kiss. White clouds softened the caress on my cheek so that when my eyes opened, the light didn't glare back at me.

It's how I woke most days here in Camelot. Unlike the rest of the United Kingdom, the sun preferred to shine here and it rarely rained. The ground was fertile, the winters mild, and the summers breezy. This place was a magical paradise, after all.

I stretched my limbs, hearing my bones and tendons crack after such a fitful rest. Funny, I know. I was about to do something wicked, and I'd had no trouble getting to sleep. I'd always been this way, even in the days when my behavior would easily be considered criminal with no tinge of heroism. I suppose I always rested easily because my conscience was so flexible.

I took a moment and wrote a note to let everyone know where I'd gone, though I'm sure they'd figure it out without the Dear John. I was sure to give a shout out to my G's. I'd looked the two men dead in their eyes and lied to them, but they were only half lies. I respected them too much to lie all the way.

I left the note on my dresser. Opening my window, I dropped my satchel outside. The pack was filled with my necessities; a change of clothes, my sword, which retracted into its magical form as a wooden walking stick, and contraceptives. A girl's gotta be prepared for everything.

With a little magic, I let the satchel sail until it softly landed on the ground at the back of the castle. I took one last look around my bedroom, feeling somewhat maudlin. But I promptly shook that feeling off. I'd be back soon with my bestie in tow and we'd be having a big girl's sleepover with Gwin and Morgan in no time. Assuming I wasn't grounded for too long.

With a quiet snick of the door, I stole out of my

bedroom and headed for the long and winding staircase that would lead me on my journey.

It was early, but this castle never slept. Already, children were racing down the halls, chasing each other, spinning spells, or hiding from their daily chores. Each and every one of them called out a "Hi, Lady Lo," or a "Good Morn, Dame Galahad."

I greeted each one in turn, asking after their parents, scolding them to watch where they were going, promising I'd play with them later. Another half-truth. I would be back *later*.

"Oh, good. You're still here."

Gwin's soft voice had me nearly jumping out of my skin. She was shutting the door to the infirmary as she headed toward me. Before the door to the sick room closed, I caught sight of Gwin's ailing husband, Merlin. The bastard was still clinging to life despite the deadly wound he'd received with a magical object months ago.

The Spear of Destiny had stripped Merlin of what powers he had left. But it was Gwin's nursing, Arthur's indulgence, and Merlin's selfishness that kept the impotent wizard breathing comfortably and safe inside the castle walls.

I felt a moment of irritation. Here, Arthur was going to great lengths to save the life of someone who had caused so much pain, even death, to his people. But he wouldn't let me go rob a deity in a forbidden realm and then steal down into the Garden of Eden to save my best friend? Hypocrite.

"I'm glad I ran into you," said Gwin.

"I was just heading down ..."

I have no idea why I paused. The half lie was prepped and ready to roll off my tongue. I was going down to the kitchen—partly true. But I would keep going out the back door and off the grounds—full truth. The words caught in my throat as I stood before my cousin.

Gwin looked at me, patiently waiting for me to finish my statement. Her lovely features held not a trace of suspicion or doubt. Her smile was question-less, sanguine, and untroubled.

When I didn't pick up the end of my sentence, or move my tongue any closer to the lie, Gwin smiled brighter and took my hand in hers. Her fingers were warm to the touch as she rested the back of my hand in her palm.

"I wanted to give you this," she said.

Gwin held a locket in her hand. She held it by a gold chain and let the circular bobble hang free. I became fixated on the piece of jewelry.

The gem was mesmerizing. My eyes volleyed

back and forth in time to its swaying. It was an inch in diameter and midnight blue. But then it brightened to indigo, then sapphire, and periwinkle. Only to darken its way back down the color spectrum.

Gwin placed the necklace in my hand. It felt like ten espresso shots fed intravenously into my blood. The locket positively hummed with power.

"What is this?" I whispered.

"Oh, just a little something I dug out of the vault," Gwin said.

My head jerked up and met a blue mirror image of my own. Those words, coming from this person, surprised the hell out of me. Had I misheard her? Had goody-two-shoes Gwin said she'd gotten the necklace from the vault?

That's where Arthur kept all the priceless artifacts. No one was allowed into the vault. Unless that someone was as trustworthy and beyond reproach as Lady Gwin.

"It's a pocket of energy," Gwin continued. "It can create a ripple through space even where there isn't enough energy for a ley line. It'll bring you somewhere safe if ever you're in a pickle."

My surprise turned into suspicion. "Why are you giving this to me, Gwin?"

There was a gleam in her light eyes. "You seem to always find yourself in pickles, my dear cousin."

I opened my mouth. But just as I couldn't form a half lie to deliver to her, neither could I spout the full truth.

It was no matter. Gwin pulled me into a fierce hug. She squeezed tight enough for liquid to pool at the corners of my eyes. But she let me go before a single drop could fall.

Gwin pulled away from me. Her face was once again set in that mask of purity and hospitality. She winked at me and then walked off without another word.

I knew she'd planned for her words of support and gift of a talisman to be helpful, but all I felt was an overwhelming sense of guilt. I felt like a complete rogue, a scoundrel, a scalawag. I felt like a person who'd spent far too much time in a medieval world that even my slang was slipping into the archaic.

I shoved the necklace into my back pocket alongside the Ring of Gyges. Now I had two misappropriated magical artifacts in my employ. With such an arsenal of protection in my favor, something was bound to go wrong.

"Good, you haven't left yet."

I rolled my eyes skyward and turned to face

Morgan. Why was I even bothering to sneak around if my destination was so clear to my family? I looked around to see if anyone else had heard her, but no one was within earshot.

"I'm not—" I began to deny my intention to leave, but the look Morgan gave me told me it was pointless.

"You can't come," I said.

The last time Morgan came with me on a quest she was the one that got hurt. If anyone was taking the blame for this, it would be me and solely me. I wouldn't be putting another innocent in danger ever again.

Not that Morgan was entirely innocent. But she hadn't deserved to be stripped of her powers by the same spear that felled Merlin. At least she was healthy and on her feet and not dying in the infirmary.

"Not asking to go," said Morgan. "Do you think either Gwin or I doubted that you were going? You'd come for us if we were lost. And we'd come for you. I just wanted to say don't get caught or trapped or killed because, as fun as it may sound, I have no desire to go to the fae realm where they fear science and technology. I'm prepping for the second annual Camelot Science Fair."

Morgan's eyes twinkled at the prospect of being surrounded by chemicals and hypotheses and pocket protectors. I could only laugh. Then I pulled her into a tight embrace. That time, a single tear did leak from my left eye, but I swiped it away before I let her go.

We parted without any more words. They weren't necessary. I gave up my attempt to sneak out and walked purposefully toward the back door.

"Loren."

Arthur's voice stopped me in my tracks. I froze, my rigid spine likely gave me away. I turned about face and tried to appear loose.

Arthur leveled his steely gaze on me. The skin between his brows wrinkled as he crossed broad arms over his chest. He took a deep breath and then released it, unfolding his arms, un-creasing his brow and softening his gaze.

"Listen," he said, "I'm sorry about Nia. Despite our checkered past, she has always been an ally to the people here in Camelot."

I shuffled forward a couple of steps. "So, you've changed your mind? You'll let me go?"

"No." He held up a finger. "It doesn't appear she's in any immediate danger. She's with her family."

"With all due respect, boss, your family is

upstairs in the infirmary after presenting a clear and present danger to everyone in this town."

"I was trying to be empathetic," Arthur said through a clenched jaw. "Let Mohandis go to the other realm and get the hammer. Then, when he gets back, we'll reassess the situation and see what personnel and resources we can lend to getting to Nia. Is that fair?"

"I don't know that it's fair?" I said. "But you're not giving me any other choice. So ..."

"I'm not the bad guy here," Arthur said.

"I know you're not the bad guy. You're a great guy. But you can be so rigid about the safety of everyone that you don't always consider their happiness. That is your flaw."

The momentary softness melted away and his features hardened in real time. Before he could say anything else, or worse, before I could say anything else, I decided to make a run for it.

"I'm gonna go get something to eat and then tend to my duties," I said.

This time, the full lie rolled easily off my tongue and landed in the space between us. Arthur backed out of my way. I walked past him and into the kitchen.

The kitchen door swung closed behind me. The

familiar scents wrapped around me, giving me the strength I needed to temporarily turn my back on this family to save my friend.

When I looked up, Igraine held out a paper bag. Grease stains wet the bottom of the sack. The foul smell wafting out of the top of the bag made my belly grumble with hunger. I took it from her, unsurprised. If no one else, of course, she'd seen me coming and preparing to go.

Igraine kissed me on the cheek and then opened the back door for me. Before I crossed the threshold, I gave her the same hug Gwin and Morgan had given me. Then, picking up my satchel along the way, I left the grounds of Camelot.

6

Getting out of the castle was a breeze, but getting to Caerleon proper was proving to be a bit of a hassle. I'd thought of saddling up my magical horse, Achila, but I couldn't parade her through the suburbs. Besides that, I had to get on a highway to get to my end destination.

The small town of Camelot might appear to be modest, but there was a lot of wealth hidden behind the medieval doors. These people and their ancestors had been around for centuries. Some family lines went back millennia. There was not a single poor person in Camelot.

That's what I kept repeating to myself as I slipped into the car parked at the Visitor's Center. No one drove on the main street of town. There was no need for witches, wizards, and knights to use such technology in close quarters. Vehicles were only used on excursions into the human world, and that's what I was doing; going on an excursion.

I slipped into the driver's seat of the unlocked car. Not only was it unlocked, the keys were sitting idly in the ignition. I'd never been a car thief, though I did know how to hotwire a car. This guy I used to know had taught me.

Now that I think back on it, he'd had a different car every time he'd come to pick me up for an evening out.

The community car purred to life. Placing my foot on the brake, I took one last look out the rearview mirror. No one was running toward me, telling me to stop. So I put the car in reverse and took off.

It had been a minute since I'd driven. It had been an age since I'd driven in Europe. Once out of town and on the main roads, I kept veering to the wrong side of the road.

Horns blared at me. Fists rose out of windows, brandishing middle fingers. I ignored the angry shouts and focused my attention on the digital clock on the car's dashboard. I was running out of time.

In fact, I was sure my time was pretty much up.

Tres had said he'd leave at sunrise. Well, there was a big, yellow disk high in the sky looking down on me.

If only I hadn't stopped and talked to my cousins, I might have saved a bit of daylight.

If only I hadn't been accosted by Arthur and his suspicious brow, I might have had a moment to spare.

If only this were a race car and not a mini wagon, I might make it to the docks before Tres sailed away.

But wait. I was a witch filled with magic. I was a knight on a quest. And this family-friendly wagon was only a pumpkin waiting to be turned into a turbocharged phaeton.

I looked at the dash and considered my options. My foot was already pressing the gas pedal into the floorboard. The speedometer's needle crested past eighty miles per hour. There had to be something more I could do.

And then I spied it. The cigarette lighter. I pulled the cap out. The metal embers glowed bright orange.

I squeezed the palm of my hand, summoning a ball of energy. I let up off the gas just a bit. Then I placed my palm over the lighter.

The car coughed as it inhaled my magical flames. Then it wheezed, slowing down further. The cars behind me in the fast lane honked at me.

Just as I was about to give up and signal right for the slower lane, the wagon shuddered. It felt as though it were being stripped of its orange exterior. I can't be sure that I saw sparks come off the hood, or if that just might have been a trick of the rising sunlight, but the car shimmied and took off like a rocket.

It felt as though the wheels were no longer touching the asphalt. The scenery along the side of the highway was a blur of Jackson Pollock slashed colors. All my concentration was on zipping in and out of the slower moving traffic because now everyone was moving much slower than me.

I thrust my fist out the window and pumped. I'd make it now. I had to at this speed. And before I knew it, there it was. The docks.

Now, I just needed to figure out how to stop the car. Braking was only slowing it down a few miles with each pump. There were no longer any cars in my way as I'd turned off the highway.

The problem was that I was running out of road. All that was left in front of me was water. Unfortunately, the car was still going forty miles an hour.

There was nothing left for me to do. I had to abandon ship. With a few more taps on the brake, I got the car slowed down to twenty miles an hour.

I grabbed my satchel. With a tug on the handle, I yanked open the car door. Water was already coming into the driver's side when I leaped out. In an instant, my body was submerged into the murky waters.

I surfaced just as a splash sounded to my right. A white dingy floated beside me. Grabbing onto it, I followed the trail of the rope it was attached to.

Tresor Mohandis pulled the other end of the rope towards a massive yacht. He was backlit by the sun. He stood at the helm in a crisp white shirt that showcased his brown muscles as they worked to pull me to him. It was a good thing I was in the water, because my entire body overheated at the sight of him.

He pulled me up with barely any effort hefting me onboard his ship. In return, I dripped murky water onto his dry floors.

"You waited," I said, my voice breathless. My eyes were waterlogged, and I had to blink a couple of times to see him clearly. "You waited for me."

"I didn't have a choice," Tres said. He steadied me on my feet and then he stepped away from me so I could see what, or rather who, took his choices away.

The water fell from my eyes and my mouth

gaped open. Behind Tres, helping themselves to his fully stocked bar sat Geraint and Gawain.

"GG?"

They both raised their glasses to me in salute as they lounged. Gerry cringed as he took me in from my toes to my head. I swiped a hand through my hair and came away with what I hoped was seaweed.

Wain held up his cell phone in the other hand. "I got that all on video. I'm posting it right now so everyone back in town can see."

"No," I held up my hands. "You can't."

Humiliation aside, if he posted that video of me driving one of the town's cars off the dock, then everyone would know where I was. My head cocked to the side, and I stared at them. But then I had to straighten my head as water sloshed around in my inner ear.

"Wait," I said. "How did you two know I'd be here?"

The two knights looked at each other in that stupid silent communication. Then looked at me, the meaning of their twin expressions clear. In unison, they smirked and snorted.

"*Pfft*," Gerry said. "You are entirely predictable. We know how that mind of yours works."

"We knew you wouldn't sit still," said Wain. "It's not in your nature."

"Plus, it's Nia," said Gerry. "You two have that whole girl bond thing."

"We knew you wouldn't let this go," said Wain. "And we wouldn't let you go alone."

I dropped my bag on the floor. It went down with a sluicing sound instead of a thud. Tres grimaced as though it had landed on his white shirt instead of the floor. I barely paid him any mind, my attention was on my fellow knights.

"Let me get this straight," I said. "You knew I was lying to you last night?"

"Of course," said Gerry. He took a sip of his drink before he continued. "We didn't buy any of that act you put on."

"So, you knew I was lying about doing something dangerous and neither of you called me on it?"

Gerry's ear twitched like he thought he heard a sound in the distance. Wain's nose wrinkled like he smelled something foul in the air.

"What's happening?" said Gerry.

"I think she's about to somehow turn this around on us," said Wain.

"Can she do that?" asked Gerry.

"Neither of you thought to call me on my lie to

my face?" I said. "And you call yourselves my friends?"

Wain scratched the back of his neck. "I think this is reverse psychology."

"Or early onset dementia on her part," said Gerry.

"Listen, Loren," said Wain. "We're your brothers, and your sister is in ..." He looked past me to Tres. "She's not exactly in mortal danger being that she already died, right?"

Tres opened his mouth to answer, but Gerry cut him off.

"I thought she couldn't die since she's an immortal being?"

"Yeah, that is a bit confusing," said Wain. "It sounded to me like she's being grounded by her deity parents."

"Well then, if that's the case," said Gerry. "I'm unclear on the moral standing here. If she's being punished by her parents, and we go in and rescue her, aren't we technically kidnapping?"

I looked at Tres. He rolled his eyes as though to say this is your mess to clean up.

"It doesn't matter," I said. "I'm going to get her. So you know you're not getting me off this boat without a fight."

I reached down and pulled out my sword with one hand. Then I ignited a fireball with the other. It took a minute as my hands were wet, but I got a pretty good spark going.

"Please don't scorch the interior," said Tres. "I just had it redone."

Geraint and Gawain made no move to get up out of their seats. In fact, they reached for the bottle they'd been nursing and poured themselves another drink.

"Did you not just hear us?" asked Gerry. "We're not dragging you back."

"We're coming with you," said Wain.

"You are?" I lowered my sword, but I didn't extinguish the flame. The heat was drying out the dregs in my clothing.

"Of course," said Wain. "You think we'd let you go out on your own?"

He downed his drink. Then he pulled out another glass, filled it, and lifted it toward me. I came to him and took the drink. I took a healthy gulp and was warmed from the inside out.

"Does Arthur know?" I asked.

Instead of answering, both men took another drink.

Crap. He did know. He had known as I lied to his

face. And yet he hadn't stopped me from coming. I reached out my glass and Gerry poured me another drink, a hefty one.

"Here's the deal," said Gerry. "We go in, we get the hammer, and we get out. No magic. If anyone in the other realm finds out what we are, it'll break the treaty. That can't happen. Understand?"

No magic? No problem.

7

_____

I made my way around Tres's luxury yacht. I already knew my way seeing as I had spent a glorious night on the boat some months ago. Tres, Nia and I had sailed from Istanbul, Turkey to Athens, Greece when we were trying to uncover the mystery of the tablet that belonged to the Greek goddess Demeter.

During that trip, I'd tried to push Nia into Tres's arms. She'd just broken up with Zane for the umpteenth time and was wallowing in misery. While she was so busy stumbling around over her broken heart, she nearly missed out on the billionaire hottie that couldn't keep his eyes off her. So, I shoved her into his arms.

Not just because I wanted to stay on his big boat,

or hop into his private jet, or ride shotgun in one of his many muscle cars. Did I mention the dude was rich?

I mainly pushed Nia toward Tres because she needed to remember that men were a dime a dozen. She needed to stop looking after the pennies and let the pounding come. She needed to rub her nickel against someone else's gold.

You bet your bottom dollar I made all those clichéd references until she ran from me and flung herself at Tres. The problem was that she wound up back in our room early that night. Unlike my own, my bestie's happiness couldn't be bought. Nia was hopeless, a lost cause, for any man who wasn't Zane.

Too bad. Tres's bed looked quite sturdy. A nice, firm mattress that could bounce a dime a couple of times. An ornate wooden headboard with columns to grasp onto in the throes of passion. And were those thousand count sheets to nestle into after sweaty sex?

I stood in the doorway of his bedroom gazing in. I wasn't invading his privacy. The door had been open. A crack. I may have given it a gentle shove (a couple of times) until it swung wide.

The interior was tastefully done in light, sandy browns and darker cocoa colors. It gave the room a warm feeling, like being cocooned inside of a hollowed out tree. The soft yellow light of the sky and the clear blue of the sea completed the color pattern from the wall of windows to one side of the room.

Between the warmth of the fixtures and the peace of the outside scenery, I couldn't imagine a reason to leave the room. But I was standing on the outside. And so I took a step inside.

The closet stood slightly ajar and I saw into his wardrobe. He was a neat freak. Everything was lined up, starched and pristine. All of his pants and shirts faced the same way, to the right of the closet. His shoes were color-coordinated from darkest to the lighter shades going left to right.

On top of a dresser were cases of cufflinks, watches, thick, manly rings that would only fit on my thumb, and an assortment of earrings made of precious stones. Again, all were in alignment and organized. The cufflinks were arranged by size. The watches by their metal components. It appeared the gemstones were organized by how precious they were.

There was a small desk where I had to assume he did business dealings. But even there, not a paper or pen out of place. Everything was neatly stacked in labeled folders—typed labeled folders, not hand-written. I wondered if I needed to set aside the title Broody Billionaire and relabel him a control freak.

And then I spotted it. One thing that didn't quite fit in place. On the bedside table, there sat a figurine. It was old, chipped, faded. It lay in an open box. The belly of the box was velvet. I wondered if that material was more precious than the stone the object was carved from. Peering closer, I began to doubt that.

It wasn't so much that the figurine was worn. It was old. It was also familiar.

It depicted an imposing man. His eyes were carved to glare. His mouth was a thin line of menace. Swirls were carved atop his head, on his face, and around his shoulders to indicate he was a hairy beast. With one arm, he clutched a roaring lion to his chest.

I scooped the piece of stone from its plush pallet. I'd seen this figure before. Perhaps in one of my dad's textbooks, or in a museum, or maybe even on the ancient walls of a temple. I couldn't place it at the moment.

Whatever it was, it was authentic. It had to be original. Tres was an ancient being. It was one of the ways he'd made his wealth, simply by saving it and putting it aside for thousands of years.

This figurine couldn't have been worth much during the time it was carved. But he'd kept it with him for centuries. I was dying to know why and what it meant to him?

I heard the loud footsteps alerting me to someone's presence. Tres hadn't taken on a crew. He'd said it was too dangerous to bring on any human lives. Only Geraint, Gawain, and I were on board with him. I knew those two knights' footfalls having lived and fought with them for months now. This had to be Tres, especially since I was in his bedroom.

I could've faced him like a grown woman. I hadn't done anything wrong. I was just nosing around his room.

So, of course, I stood tall ... and dashed into his super-organized closet. Shimmying my way amongst the hung cloth, I made a mess of his pants. Two pairs fell off their hangers and to the floor at my feet.

Tres came through the opened door. He stepped over the threshold, then paused. He glanced back at the door, looking from the door jamb. His gaze swept the distance to the frame. He blinked, his lids narrowing as though he sensed something. His brow creased. And then, just as suddenly, all the tension that had gathered in his features released.

Leaving the door wide open, Tres turned and

faced the mirror. He reached for the top button of his shirt and slipped it through the clasp. The skin just below his clavicle was revealed. Well, what of his skin I could see. It was mostly covered by a dark smattering of hair; the same hair that lightly coated his neck and strong jaw.

Tres reached for the next button and did the same, slipping it through the button hole and revealing more brown skin and dark swirls of hair. And then the next, and the next until the shirt hung from his body and revealed his entire, defined, rock hard chest.

It was the first non-brotherly chest I'd seen in a while. So I gaped. How could I not? It was there, and big, and broad, and bitable.

Yes, bitable. I wanted to sink my teeth into the fleshy part just there beneath his right pectoral where his silky mat of hair neglected to touch. I'd be more than willing to give it some attention.

Wait. What? No.

I couldn't have these thoughts. This was my bestie's ex. Although they hadn't actually consummated anything this time around in their relationship. Their last boinking couldn't have been within the last five hundred years, which might make my gaping within bounds. There had to be some statute of limitations on the girl code. Right?

With back dimples like that there just had to be a loophole. The muscles at Tres's shoulder blades rippled around his spine. Twin depressions appeared just above his waistline. I swallowed and dug my fingers into my palms. But I only felt my nails go into one palm.

I looked down to see the obstruction. It was the figurine. I still had it in my hands. Then I thought back to the trajectory of Tres's gaze when he'd come in. He'd looked at the empty box. He knew I was in here.

"I'm guessing you strip for all your guests?" I said.

"Nope." He didn't jump at the sound of my voice. He barely even glanced up. "Just the ones who like to play voyeuristic thief."

Tres reached for the waistband of his slacks. He slipped the button through the buttonhole. Then his fingers clasped the zipper.

"You can stop now," I said as I came out of the closet.

He didn't. He let his pants slip down his hips and pool on the floor. His toes peeked out from under the fabric. Yes, I was looking at his feet and not his package. I was trying to maintain some morsel of decorum.

Tres walked past me. My sense of decency crumbled as he did so. I snuck a peek and was handsomely rewarded. Ever the warrior, he was all commando.

I didn't get a good look at his package as his behind was facing me as he reached into his closet. As he shifted his weight to pick up the pants that had fallen in my hiding spot, and to place the pants and shirt he was discarding into a bin, I saw the tip of his manhood. Well, what of it I could see. He was uncircumcised.

"Is that your kink?" I asked, genuinely curious. "Being watched?"

Tres slipped a clean shirt over his head. It fell down until it covered all but the bottom half of his cheeks. "I doubt you're here to seduce me. Best friend code or girly promises or sisterhood bond or whatever."

"Exactly," I agreed, swallowing hard on the single word.

Tres stepped into his pants legs. Then he turned and eyed me. The sound of the zipper teeth closing him in the only sound in the room. Well, aside from my carefully shallow breaths that were doing nothing but making me lightheaded.

"What do you want, Loren?"

"I want ..." Don't say *you*. Don't say *you*.

Tres tucked his shirt into his waistband and came toward me. There wasn't much space in the large suite, but I felt like he was rising up over a dune to come and swoop me up and onto his Arabian steed. But then he stalked right past me, leaving me feeling dry-mouthed and parched.

He went over to his bed. He looked at the mattress. Then he looked at me.

My cheeks heated. Not with embarrassment. No, when I got embarrassed, I went cold. My cheeks only ever heated when I couldn't deny that I wanted something.

Tres cleared his throat with impatience. The flush spread to my neck. It was threatening to creep over my breasts. My nipples were already firm points beneath my shirt.

I made a move to lift my foot. Was I seriously about to do this? To go to him? To give my body to him. You bet your-

Tres reached over to the bed stand and snatched up the empty box. He pushed it towards me expectantly. The heat left my body in a cold gust.

He hadn't been eyeing the bed. He'd been eyeing the bed stand. He wasn't beckoning me to put my body in his bed. He was beckoning me to put his figurine back in the box from which I took it.

"I was just looking," I said as I reached out my hand and dropped the ancient piece back in its place.

"I'm sure that's what you were doing with my pants too." Tres snapped the box shut.

"Ew," I protested. "I'm not some pervert. Well, I am. But not like that."

"I assume you want to speak with me about your fellow knights?" he said, crossing his arms over his chest.

Who? Oh, right. Geraint and Gawain.

"Are you also thinking of tossing them over before we hit the high seas?" asked Tres.

"What? No. We're not tossing them over. They're my brothers."

"Brothers?" Tres's voice was hard as he looked down at the closed box in his hand. "People toss that word around even when they don't share blood, like it means something."

"It does mean something," I insisted.

"I thought Zane and I were brothers. Look where

that got me." Tres shoved the box in the bed stand drawer and then slammed the drawer shut.

"Um, aren't you the one that tried to steal his girlfriend?" I asked.

Tres looked up at me, affronted.

I held up my hands. "Hey, I was Team Broody Billionaire all the way."

"I do not brood." He loomed over me, his mood darkening the light in his eyes.

"Whatever you say. But you did break the bro code."

Tres threw up his hands and stalked to the window. The sea stretched out before us as far as the eye could see. The boat rocked gently as we made our way to the other side of the planet toward the Caribbean. The turbulence of his muscles bunched beneath the light fabric of his shirt.

"You know," he said, "there really is no such thing as a brotherhood code. Not written down anyway."

"That's why it's sacred. It's a bunch of unwritten rules." I walked over to the window and joined him. "And they're not a secret, everyone knows them. Thou shalt not put a hoe over a bro being rule number one."

Tres scowled. But not at me. Not even at the blue

sea. In the clear glass of the window, his reflection glared back at him.

"Thou shalt be loyal to your bro," I continued. "Thou bros' sisters, mamas, and exes are all off limits. A bro is brutally honest with his bro. And a bro always protects his bro."

I looked up at Tres's pained face and realized he'd broken every one of those rules where it came to Zane. Tres wasn't looking at his reflection anymore. His gaze was over his shoulder, locked on the closed drawer that housed the figurine.

I no longer wondered what the figurine meant. I was pretty sure who'd made it. Zane was an artist of many mediums, carving and sculpture were one of the many.

"You're right," I said, trying to backpedal my earlier comments. "There's nothing written in stone about brothers. Not like the Commandments or the Constitution."

Tres didn't rally. His shoulders slumped. He turned from me and leaned his back against the window.

"Besides," I continued, "you're risking your neck to save both Zane and Nia now."

"I will get them back," he vowed. "Then I'll leave them alone. I've proven I can't keep the bro code.

She will never look at me the way she looks at him. Hell, she died for him. Game over, right? I lose."

I opened my mouth. Then closed it. I had no more witty quips for him.

"And still," he continued, "there's a part of me that hopes that when I rescue her, she'll choose me."

"It's not stupid to want to be chosen."

I laid my hand on his shoulder. I could feel his warm flesh through his thin shirt. I had the strangest impulse to rub my thumb back and forth. I found myself giving into it. It wasn't much, but it was the only comfort I had to offer him since he obviously had no interest in taking me to bed.

Not that I would've gone in the first place. That had just been a moment of insanity. I had my wits about me again. I saw the truth of the matter.

"You're not the villain," I said the truth out loud because I wasn't sure if he knew it himself.

Tres looked at me then. I saw my own reflection in his eyes. I also saw the same doubt in his eyes that I still felt over that very statement about myself.

8

_I_ left Tres's room and climbed back to the main deck. As I came to the top of the stairs, the fresh sea air hit me like a slap in the face. What the hell had just happened?

I'd been alone in a room with a naked man; a handsome, rich, well-endowed, powerful, naked man. And we didn't end up in bed together. I was so confused about my life choices right now.

Nia owed me. Big time. This friendship was costing me more than I was willing to pay at the moment.

Nia and I regularly shared clothes. I had a couple pairs of her pants stashed in my drawers back in Camelot. And I think this was her shirt I'd changed into after my untimely swim. These definitely were her boots. And the lip gloss I'd coated my lips with this morning was also on loan from her. Though I was pretty sure I was keeping it since it looked way better with my fair coloring than it did on her.

Even with all the many things we shared, there was a sense of fairness to it. I took the things she no longer wanted. Or she didn't realize I now held them in my possession. Right now, Tresor Mohandis was one of those unrealized things.

The truth is that Nia had never truly wanted him. She didn't realize right now that he was with me. Not *with* me, but in my proximity and feeling vulnerable enough to want to share some of his pain.

Damn. I was still grasping for loopholes.

I heard a male throat clear. I whirled around, thinking that maybe Tres had rethought asking me to leave his room and wanted to take the few steps to his bed. I was wrong. On so many levels, yes, I know.

When I turned, I found myself face to face with the G's. The two men looked nothing alike but their expressions were that of Siamese twins. Suspicion, condemnation, disappointment, expectation.

The stairwell that I ascended from only led to one place, to Tres's bedroom.

"We ..." I began. And then, "I ..." My arms crossed

over my chest and I glared back at them. "Do I really need to explain this?"

They both glared back, telling me that I did.

"He's not into me." The man had undressed in front of me without girding his loins. Or pointing them in my direction. "He's in love with my best friend."

That evidence didn't sway either of the G's. Should I tell them about the naked, non-pointing part? Probably not, if I didn't want a mutiny aboard the ship.

"There's a code," I finally settled on. What had Tres called it? Oh, right. "A sisterhood bond. I can't break it or my periods will unsync and I will never be able to borrow an emergency tampon again."

That did it. The two valiant knights groaned their horror and broke ranks. Geraint shuddered. Gawain clutched at his stomach.

Men. They could discuss their own bowel movements, flatulence, itches and scratches. But mention the wonders of nature that occurs within a woman's vagina, when it doesn't concern them, and they become adolescents.

"Still," said Gerry after he'd shaken off his distaste. "He's a man. You're a woman. You're both mourning the loss of a lover."

"And you've said it yourself, my lady," said Wain. "The best way to get over someone is to get under someone else."

I had not said that. "I said the best way to get over someone is to get on top of someone else. Why would a sane person choose the submissive position?"

"We just don't want him toying with your heart," said Gerry. "A guy like that and a girl like you?"

A cold sweat broke out on my brow. It sent a chill down my spine. I fought to lift my gaze to Geraint and keep the tremor out of my voice. "What does that mean, *a girl like me*?"

"It's really him I'm referring to," Gerry glared down the empty stairwell. Then he lifted his arms to sweep over the deck of the yacht. "Look at this boat. Mohandis is a playboy. He likes the finer things."

I wrapped my arms around myself and rubbed, trying to create warmth. "Are you saying I'm not a fine thing?"

Gerry tilted his head to the side. His features were screwed as though he had not a clue as to what I was referring to.

"I am a bona fide lady, you know."

I balled my hand into a fist. Witch fire burned in my palms, but the warmth didn't reach beyond my hands. My teeth were clenched without the chattering. My shoulders were bunched up to my ears even though it was warm beneath the sun's rays.

"Of course, you are," said Gerry. He straightened his head, holding his chin high, and frowning at me. He looked angry as he regarded me. "And that's why I won't let Mohandis trifle with you."

Slowly the cold began to leave my body and warmth filtered back in. "You won't let *him* trifle with *me*."

Sir Geraint held up a finger in warning. "Don't even start this argument with me, Loren. I know better than to boss you around by now. It only steers you in the wrong direction."

No, it did not. I took the final step to bring me onto the deck with the guys and out of the path back toward Tres's bedroom. It took an extra couple of seconds for my fingers to release the handrail.

"Mohandis is the type of guy to pounce when opportunity strikes," Gerry continued. "Not only are you beautiful, smart, and strong, you're all the things any man wants."

I failed to catch my lower lip when it went slack. That couldn't be true. Men wanted beautiful, sure. But smart and strong? Didn't that contradict with their own self-importance?

"You're feeling vulnerable right now," said Gerry. "Any man, especially one like Mohandis, can smell that. We won't leave you alone with him so he can strike."

"Oh," I sighed, as Gerry took me under his arm and pulled me away from the stairs. "That's really ... just great."

"I'll tell you one thing," said Wain. "The man might be a scoundrel. But it sure pays better than being a knight."

"Being a knight pays in goodwill," said Gerry.

"So says the wealthy prince," said Wain.

I turned to Wain and pointed my thumb at Gerry. "You know he's only here to get another glimpse at Enid, that purple fae girl I told you about."

"The one that bound him in vines and thorns?" said Wain.

"And somehow I'm the one that gets the kinky label?" I said.

Gerry turned to me. His skin was too dark to turn red, but he had all the telltale signs of being caught red-handed. "That's not—I'm not—"

"What's the matter, big guy?" I snickered. "Vine got your tongue?"

Geraint reached for me. I ducked behind Gawain and stuck out my tongue. Wain spread his arms to protect me, but he was laughing so hard he didn't move with me as Gerry reached around him.

I swiveled around my human shield but found myself cornered between the boat's railing and the might of a charging knight. There was nowhere to run. But I didn't need to escape. Not when the assault was a huge bear hug.

Gerry caught me and brought me in for one of his stiff hugs. They really weren't so bad. The affection was all in the thought if not the execution.

"You're my brother," he said. "But one day, I'm probably going to strangle you."

"Not if I squeeze the life out of you first." I tried to then. I squeezed him as hard as I could, but it only made him chuckle and squeeze me tighter.

I relaxed in his hold and looked to the side at Wain. "You guys came after me, even after I said I wouldn't come."

"Well," said Wain. "You didn't say you *wouldn't* come. Which is how we knew you would come. We listened."

Damn. Was I really that transparent? Or maybe they were just my true brothers, able to read my own sister code.

I stepped out of Gerry's hold, lowering my arms to my side. When I did, my hand brushed my pocket and the slight indent there. The Ring of Gyges burned me from the inside. I opened my mouth to say something, but the G's weren't done.

"You're loyal to Nia," said Gerry. "And we know you'd never put anyone in Camelot in harm's way."

"It's one for all," said Wain.

"Just like the Three Musketeers." I clasped my hands to my chest in delight. But both men reared back and shook their heads like I was about to start talking about my menstrual cycle again.

"We are not wearing feathered hats," said Gerry.

"Oooh," I crooned. "But they'd go so well with your full eyelashes."

"No," they both said in unison.

Fine. Whatever. They could think that for now. I'd work on their fashion senses later.

9

I liked boats. I really did. But this is the second time this year that I'd been in a major storm that set the boat a'rocking.

The yacht thrashed about like an angry god was trying to rip it to shreds. I called on Psi, but apparently, the Greek god didn't hear my pleas outside of the Mediterranean Sea. I also called on Vivi, but the sea witch had been quiet of late. No one knew where she'd got to.

Tres and the G's rushed about trying to maintain their control of the vessel. I'd come below to grab my pack as well as the knights' stuff in case we had to abandon ship. I was headed back up but took a detour into Tres's room to grab what I could. That's when the boat really took a beating.

I was quite happy to stay below and grip Tres's bedpost. Though it wasn't what I'd had in mind when I'd dreamed of laying in his bed with my hands wrapped around the post. My head banged the headboard in repetitive motion. This was not arousing. It was terrifying.

He'd taken the figurine out of the drawer since I was last in here. The box on his bed stand fell to the floor and the figurine popped out. I reached down for it and took it in my grasp. At that very moment, we hit rough seas, and I tumbled off the bed.

All had been calm on the seas every day of the journey up until now. I'd spent the days in bliss. I'd lounge on the deck in a bikini I'd procured from the wardrobe. It was new, likely meant for the parade of floozies Tres was known to have in his entourage during his time as a playboy.

I'd watched the sunrise, the waves rolling in an endless blue. I'd worked out in the crew's quarters on the Bowflex with Geraint and Gawain. We also watched movies in the bar, got drunk in the bar, and played video games in the bar.

We three were having a grand old time. It was like a vacation. I'd almost forgot that we were in a time crunch.

I forgot what land, mountains, buildings, civilization looked like, and I did not miss it. There wasn't a single day of rough weather as we crossed the Atlantic Ocean. Even when it was predicted, the weather was never as bad as anticipated. We'd see the oncoming storms a mile away from us, but they never touched us. It was like someone was watching over us, easing our way toward our destination. It should've taken five weeks at sea. We were approaching the Caribbean in under three.

Tres had kept scarce. Most of his days were spent on the bridge doing yacht stuff. He never touched alcohol, unlike his wayward crew of three. He kept a polite distance from us, even though we all invited him with genuine come-join-us waves. But he preferred to keep himself apart. Clearly, he was focused on his mission to save Nia.

The storm hit us without warning when we entered the Sargasso Sea. The sea was near the Tropic of Cancer. Our first indication that something was wrong was when the internet went out.

Before that, I'd been Snapchatting with Gwin and Morgan daily. I took pictures of the ridiculous luxury yacht. I'd even managed a few shots of Tres with his shirt off at the helm. Unfortunately, I couldn't fulfill Morgan's request to get him with his shirt off and his captain's hat on. During my fifth apology to my cousin about my failings, the connection started buffering.

Tres's money afforded him the best bandwidth. When things slowed down, I felt a prickle of awareness and looked up at the horizon. It was the first time I'd seen a cloud in weeks.

The network slowed, and then it cut out. Screens monitoring the weather went out. We didn't need the screens to see the storm barreling toward us.

With a momentary lull in the storm, I made my way back on deck. There had been a flurry of activity as the men rushed about when I'd gone below. Now the three of them stood stock still.

"That wasn't there before," said Tres pointing out toward the horizon.

The storm raced toward us with fast-forward speed. It was a funnel out of Kansas racing toward Oz. It barely touched the water as it hurtled toward us.

"It's unnatural," said Gawain.

"It must be the work of the gods," said Geraint.

"That's what we wanted," I said. "Right?"

Thunder cracked causing the boat to shake. Water crashed onto the deck. It sloshed up the sides and stayed onboard.

Overhead, I heard screams. More like squawks.

"Is that a seagull?" I asked. "Doesn't that mean we're close to land?"

"That's not a seagull," said Tres. "It's an albatross." He regarded the bird with dread.

"What's wrong?" I asked.

"Sailors believe that an albatross is a bad omen," said Wain.

Tres looked down as water sloshed at his boots. "The ship is low. Water is coming through the grills on the floor."

The waves around us rose high, over ten meters or so. The blue skies turned gray. The wind took on a biting chill. The boat began tossing and turning. I stood in the center of the deck, but my body still swayed side to side.

My feet were wet. I was in boots, but the water came up several inches. I'd been in sandals and bare feet for weeks and never got wet unless I was washing up in the bathroom.

"Loren," called Tres. "Get the ditch bags."

"You're thinking of abandoning ship?"

"Something must be wrong with the pump," said Tres.

"I'll go down," said Wain. When Tres went to warn him, Wain only shrugged. "I'll be fine. This isn't how I'm meant to die."

"You might be fine," said Gerry. "Mohandis could weather this storm. But what about me and Loren?"

Wain opened his mouth to answer, but the ship canted over to one side. We all reached out and grabbed hold of whatever we could. With aching slowness, the yacht finally rolled back. When it righted itself, only Tres and I were on deck.

I looked down and saw Geraint and Gawain falling into an abyss that had opened up in the turbulent sea. A whirlpool sucked them down so fast I didn't have time to react. A scream rose in my chest, but my mouth filled with water.

Something tugged at me. I felt arms around me. It was Tres.

"I got you," he said.

I couldn't answer. I could only cough up what seawater I hadn't swallowed. My brain was too busy trying to comprehend the absence of the G's.

Tres might've had me, but the water was trying to rip us apart. It felt like the boat was taking a nose dive. But we weren't submerged. We were going down a drain, riding the spiraling waves.

I wrapped my arms around Tres tight. If this was the way I had to go, it wasn't so bad. I was gonna die in the arms of a handsome, rich man. It was exactly the way I always wanted to go. Too bad I didn't get to spend his money or take his body out for a spin first.

But, hey, why not.

I tilted my head back and looked into Tres's eyes. Silent communication said he knew what I was thinking. Tres pressed his forehead to mine and exhaled.

No, he didn't know what I was thinking.

I was thinking my best friend was a fool for not choosing him. Sure, there were the good looks and piles of money. He may not have died *with* her like Zane had, but Tres was willing to die *for* her. What I wouldn't give for devotion like that just once in my life.

Well, no time like the present. Here I was wrapped in his arms, about to die. I slanted my mouth over his.

10

———

He didn't kiss me back.

I was too scared to pull away. My heart was pounding too hard to let him go. The energy between us so palpable I could hear it humming.

Wait, no. That was the necklace Gwin had given me. With my eyes closed, I could see the energy dancing, aching to be set free. But it wasn't as warm as Tres's lower lip.

My mind was set and my lips were locked. If he didn't want this, if he didn't want me, he'd have to do the work of disentangling my hands, arms, and legs —yes, I'd managed to wrap my legs around his waist. It was for his protection so we didn't get separated and drown.

I'd already lost my two brothers to that void. Now, I could feel it pulling at my back. In defiance, I held onto Tres for dear life.

What was I saying? Oh yes, it would have to be Tres that untangled me and pushed me away. But he didn't.

Still, he didn't kiss me back. He just held still while I kissed him. He let me nibble on his lower lip. He let me tug at his upper lip. He let me cradle his strong chin and sip at his parted lips. He let me deepen the kiss and take a gulp.

And so I did. I gulped him down. He was a dark, rich spirit, and I was a dying woman.

The taste of him drowned out my fears and washed away my sorrows. Cold water pelted my cheeks, but the droplets evaporated the second they touched my warm skin. Desire mixed with embarrassment and was shaken with a dash of devil-may-care. It was a heady experience.

So heady, I thought I imagined it when Tres's lower lip brushed against my upper lip. A touch of moisture traveled sideways unlike any raindrop I'd ever come in contact with. All around me, a storm raged, but I was in the eye of Tresor Mohandis.

He looked down at me and everything froze. I felt safe, content, as the boat tossed and turned. I didn't feel the need to dig my nails into his shirt to hold him to me. Neither of us was going anywhere in the middle of this shipwreck. I was perfectly happy to sit on his lap under his cool gaze while the world burned.

Tres's hands came on either side of my hips as though to lift me. I took a swipe at him with my tongue before he pushed me away. But it was a pull instead of a push.

My boobs squished into his firm chest. Like the good girls they were, my nipples tightened and pushed back, determined to show him who was the boss.

He pressed one hand into the small of my back. Heat spread in five different directions, radiating from his long fingers, but concentrated in his palm. My soft belly met his hard abs, and I conceded this battle.

Something clicked into place. Some unnameable thing. Actually, no. It was the boom; the pole that attached to the mast of the yacht. The boom came crashing down, but even that didn't split us apart.

Tres covered my mouth with his, tasting my upper and lower lip at once. I held still for him. My final prayer in this life was that he liked what he tasted. And, of course, it was my very last prayer that God chose to answer.

Tres let out a deep growl. I knew the sound of male satisfaction when I heard it. He licked at the seam of my lips. He didn't have to knock before I opened wide and let him in.

With his free hand, he tugged at my right thigh. My core came flush with his groin. I got pissed at my best friend for not giving me these kinds of details. Mohandis entities was a massive enterprise that covered a lot of ground.

I got greedy. I sent up another prayer, begging for a few moments more to get him undressed and welcome him inside.

But, of course, that was asking too much. Lightning struck. The boat shook, breaking us apart. Tres reached for me. His big palm wide. His long fingers grasping.

I slipped through his clutches.

I was falling. Down into the dark void, I went. I tumbled ass over head. My hands reached out and grabbed a whole lot of nothing. I fell for hours, days, years. The fall pulled all the water from my clothes, leaving me dry.

Somehow, I landed on my feet. Boots planted on firmament, I opened my eyes to see that I was inside

... something. My vision was too hazy to discern the structure. When my eyes finally adjusted, I gasped at the site before me.

I had been to the Great Barrier Reef in Australia. The bright, colorful coral structures were the most beautiful marine life I'd ever seen. The complex I stood in now was built of multi-colored electric blues, vibrant purples, and ripe oranges. The clustered polyps forged together to make towers and crevices and domes. These were homes.

No, it was a palace. A coral castle under the sea.

I saw the sea spread out before me in an endless blue. It was like looking out through one of those bottomless tour boats, but the glass wasn't just at the bottom. It was up and to the left and to the right. It was all around me.

A noise, like someone shuffling, sounded to my right. I turned and came face to face with a man. He was easily eight feet tall with white hair atop his head and a white beard at his chin. His skin was the soft gray of a dolphin's back. But it wasn't skin. Instead of flesh, he had scales. They shimmered as they caught the light turning from soft gray to teal.

"Welcome, my dear," he said. His voice was high-pitched instead of deep. "So glad you could join us. I am Aegir, God of the Sea."

I wondered if he knew Psi? But the sea was a pretty big place. More than enough room for one god to rule it.

"You're just in time," Aegir smiled.

"Just in time for what?" I asked.

"For the banquet. Look, my dear, another guest."

I turned to see a woman approaching. She was just as tall as Aegir. Long, white hair flowed down her back. She had the same shimmering scales, but hers were an array of red hues from light blush to bloody ruby.

The two beings favored each other. However, something about their body language screamed lovers instead of siblings. Still, they could be both. I'd spent a fair amount of time with the Olympians to know.

"This is my wife, Ran," said Aegir. "She is the one who welcomed you into our hall."

I wanted to question what he meant by 'welcome.' The sight of the golden net in Ran's hands gave me a clue. Bedtime stories were swirling in my head. The names Aegir and Ran bubbled up to the forefront.

Yes, Ran and Aegir. The Norse gods of the sea. Aegir was the consummate host who threw legendary parties under the blues of the ocean.

While Ran, his wife, was feared by sailors as she had a habit of casting her net and capturing the men and their treasures to horde in her underwater castle.

"This human is not a guest," said Ran. "She's a gift for our guest. Just like the others and that boat."

Others? Boat? Tres. Geraint. Gawain.

"Where are they?" I demanded.

My palm burned with fire. But I doused it before it could ignite. These were gods, Norse gods. Just the types of beings who weren't supposed to know someone like me had crossed into this realm. Not if I wanted to get what I'd come for and get out with my friends, all while keeping the treaty between this realm and Camelot.

I may have been caught, but I didn't plan to remain that way for long. I'd get out of here. It was just two gods under a glass dome, ten thousand leagues under the sea, against me. I liked my odds.

"On second thought," said Ran, "I think we'll keep this one. We can give her to our girls as a maid."

Say what now? I was being relegated to domestic goddess. I didn't think so.

Before I could call up any magic, before I could reach for my sword, before I could even voice a witty comeback, Ran's golden net ensnared me and everything went black.

11

When I opened my eyes again, I was in another opulent room made of organic material. The porous limestone formed recesses in the walls like book nooks. Each nook was large enough to fit a twin-sized bed made of sea moss. There were nine such alcoves with beds covered in spun silk of different colors. It was the tenth alcove that stood off to the side that caught my attention.

On a top shelf, there were thick scrolls rolled up and bound with leather straps. In the light of the phosphorescent blue-green algae that clung to the cubbyhole's ceiling, gems gleamed, glimmered, and glowed with a vibrance that let me know they weren't paste.

However, all of that paled in comparison to the rack of clothes at the center of the closet. Silk fabric gowns of soft pastel colors hung in the alcove. And when I say hung, I mean they floated, lightly billowing in waves of nonexistent liquid. No wire hangars to be seen.

Heart shaped bodices and flowing mermaid skirts were the design of all the dresses. Though they all were formed the same, there was so much variety that the wearer could never be accused of donning the same dress twice.

I momentarily forgot about my captivity and reached out to touch. Maybe I'd gotten it wrong. Maybe when the sea goddess, Ran, said I'd be a maid, she meant that I would work my fingers to the bone modeling this exquisite wardrobe. If so, I could conceive of staying for a while.

I picked up a sea-green dress. It shimmered from green to blue and back again in the light. I noted it was only a skirt. The top was a set of two large sea shells. The two C-cup sized shells were linked together by a string of pearls that wrapped around, like a bra.

Hunh? Fishtail skirts? Seashell bras? In an underwater castle? I knew I was missing something right in front of my face, but I couldn't put my finger on it. Probably because my hands were too busy grabbing at the clothing.

With my hands and mind preoccupied, it nearly escaped my notice that someone was approaching. I turned and looked out the glass that surrounded the cavern. A group of figures swam toward me. They had the heads, arms, and torsos of women. Their boobs were uncovered and perky breasts pointed their way to the cavern. Their lower bodies were fanning fishtails, undulating in the deep ocean as they torpedoed toward me.

Mermaids.

As they approached, the glass melted around them, separating the air and the water apart. Their scales melted away and the women stepped onto sturdy, shaven, shapely legs. I couldn't help but notice they were all Brazilian-bare down there.

Their only hair was on top their head. They all had white hair like Aegir and Ran, but different colors were woven through the girls' hair. These must be their daughters.

Each girl was over six feet tall with hourglass curves that made me jealous. One girl with teal blue streaks in her hair shoved another girl with salmon pink streaks.

"Out of my way, Bylgja," said Blue Streak.

"You stepped on my fin, Helfring." Bylgja bent down and rubbed the scales of her still transforming ankle.

"If you think he'll choose your big flipper to wife," sneered Helfring, "you're the silliest guppy in the sea."

The two mermaids chased and swatted at each other. The others set about getting dressed and jeweled up. No one paid any attention to me.

"I'm wearing the coral, Himmy," said a mermaid with lilac purple streaks. She tugged a coral pink dress out of the hands of a girl with apricot tresses amidst the white strands. "It doesn't go with your scales."

"Like he'd want you, Unnr. You're as big and brawn as a Valkyrie."

"Really," said the smallest mermaid of the bunch. Her tone was level and pleading, like a diplomat standing in the middle of two erratic dictators. She had black streaks in her hair. "We're sisters. Shouldn't we be supporting each other instead of tearing each other down?"

The mermaids all paused, eyes bugging out like goldfish. Then collectively, they shimmered their scales as they rolled their big eyes, snorted, and went back to their respective catfish fights.

The small one sighed, and her eyes rolled to me. She looked at the gown in my hands. Then she smiled and reached out.

"Thank you," she held out her arms.

I looked to the glass where breathable air met leagues of water. I had been known to hold my breath for three minutes underwater. That wasn't likely long enough for me to break the surface, with the dress in tow, and nine vicious mermaids swimming after me.

Fine. Still, my steps were hesitant, as were my fingers in unclenching the soft fabric. I reluctantly slipped the gown over her head.

"You're new," she said as she turned, indicating that I should affix the straps of the shell bra.

Instead of answering, I took each strand in hand and tugged to tie the knot.

"I'm Bara. Do you have a name?"

"Loren. I'm Loren."

"We haven't had a human attendant in over a decade. Not since mother downed an aeroplane. But there were only males onboard. I'm happy to have a female. I hope your wreck wasn't too traumatizing?"

Sweet. I'd bagged the captor with a conscience. I'd twist her good heart to my advantage to help me find the guys and get out of here. I just needed to figure out how to play it to get her to reveal anything about Tres, Geraint, and Gawain.

"You must've come in with the males mother caught earlier."

Well, that was easy. "Do you know where they are?"

"They'll be in the banquet hall waiting for his arrival."

"Whose arrival?"

In answer, thunderous quaking shook the room. An electric zap sizzled through the air. The glass of the enclosed room tinkled and bubbles formed, pressing in on the enclosure. Those sounds paled in comparison to the mermaids' squeals of delight.

"He's here!"

The ground shook again as the daughters stampeded, stomping their dainty human feet and racing from the room. I followed Bara out. She was the only one not running at a breakneck speed. We made our way back into the hall I'd fallen into upon my arrival. And there he was.

Standing in the hall was a golden god. Over seven feet tall and broad. His massive chest was covered in golden armor, but his bronze biceps were on display.

Beefcake was not apt to describe him. His right

bicep alone would swallow a cow in a choke hold. Thick, red hair covered his head down to his shoulders and a beard touched the tip of his chest. Most magnificently, there was a shining hammer in his hand.

12

"Welcome, mighty Thor," said Aegir in his high-pitched voice. "You are most welcome."

"Welcome? Or captive?" Thor's voice was a deep baritone. It reached inside the core of a drum and made the bass tremble. "I was on my way back from Jotunheim, after a successful battle against the Frost Giants, when I was felled by a net."

Thor tossed the ragged, golden threads of a net at Ran's feet. Though his voice shook the room like thunder, he didn't appear angry. His thick brow was raised in an amused kind of wariness.

"How else could we expect you to take our dinner invitation?" said Aegir. He showed not an ounce of fear in the face of the large thunder god. Instead, the sea god looked just as jovial as when he'd welcomed me into captivity.

"It's all for your own benefit, we assure you." Ran rubbed at the armor that covered Thor's chest. Her back was to her husband so Aegir didn't see the salacious smile that cut her lips. "You must celebrate your accomplishments."

"That's what I was headed back to Asgard to do." Thor grasped Ran's hand, removing it from the nipples of his chest armor. He kissed her hand and then stepped away from her.

"You would be celebrating with your men," said Ran. "What you need is the comfort of a woman."

"The mighty Valkyrie are in Asgard," said Thor. "They were preparing a victory feast at their hall to celebrate my triumph."

Ran sniffed as though Valkyrie didn't count as women.

"Partake of a meal with me and my family before you return," said Aegir. He led Thor over to the banquet of food laid out on a large table that looked as though it were made from the bones of a great whale.

"I suppose I can spare some time for a repast," said Thor as he set down his hammer. It landed with a mighty thunk that rattled the dishes on the table. "Ran, I trust I'll leave with the treasures I came with?"

"We hope you'll leave with a treasure of our own," she answered.

Thor smiled politely. I was certain I saw a trapped look in his eyes. But he kept hold of his smile as Ran called forth her long line of daughters. My eyes were locked on the hammer on the floor as Ran began the introduction of her nine daughters and all attention went to them.

I could sneak around and pick up that hammer easily, couldn't I? No one would notice me, an insignificant little human captive. Hell, I could even call the magical tool with my own power. I was getting better and better at levitation.

As I was making my retrieval plans, a flash of something else caught my eye. There was more gold netting on the floor in the corner. And the net was moving. It was moving because the bounty beneath the netting was alive.

There were three bodies caught in the net. Three men in particular; my men. Gawain, Geraint, and Tres were snared in the golden net. They were silently waving their hands to get my attention now that the gods' backs were turned away from them.

Well, this night was getting more and more

convenient. There was an unattended magical hammer in one corner, and my companions in another. I waved my hands in a jerky come-hither motion, trying to tell them to get out of the net now so we could grab our bounty and go.

Wain grabbed the netting that surrounded them. He held up two loops connected by a knot and gave it a yank. The knot didn't budge. He looked pointedly at me and yanked again. He let the unbroken knot fall and lifted his palms. The movement clearly indicating that that tactic was not working.

Okay. Made sense, it was magical and strong enough to bring down a boat, a plane, and a god. What next?

The netting didn't go beneath them, just to the floor at their feet. I made a lifting motion to indicate they should grab for the bottom and lift it up.

Now it was Gerry's turn to roll his eyes. He lifted the net from the bottom. His muscles bulged, but the net didn't budge. His pointy brow quirked up at me waiting sarcastically for my next brilliant idea.

I bit at the inside of my lip, considering options. Then my eyes lit with an obvious idea. I cradled my right wrist with my left hand. With my open hand, I lifted my index finger, pointing it at the net and making a slicing motion.

Three pairs of eyes narrowed in confusion at me. Gerry put up his hand, thumb and index finger extended. He tapped his thumb against the side of his index finger, like a hammer cocking a gun.

I shook my hands and my head. Why the heck would he think I meant gun? Knights didn't carry guns. And what good would that do against a rope? I made the motion again, slashing in a figure eight over my body.

Gerry pulled his imaginary trigger again and then opened his palms to show me his empty, gunless hands. Wain scrubbed at his temple as he shook his head at me. Tres ran his hands through his hair in frustration.

Seriously, how was he getting gun from this hand motion? I clearly didn't have my thumb cocked. This time, when I made the motion, I wrapped my hand around my hip, imitating the act of pulling a sword from a side holster. Then, for good measure, I drew my hands from behind my back, mimicking the motion of unsheathing a sword from a back holster.

The men looked at each other, impatience clear on their faces. They each turned and gave me their backs and then their sides. Their swordless backs and sheathless hips.

When they turned back around, Wain mouthed *duh.*

Well, how was I supposed to know they were weaponless? Aegir and Ran hadn't bothered to relieve me of my satchel. It still hung at my side.

I held up my hands to indicate what next?

A witch, two knights, and an immortal walk into a banquet hall. It sounded like the start of a raunchy joke. The guys weren't laughing. In fact, Gerry's annoyance had transformed into a look of dread.

I followed his gaze to see that Ran's presentation of her daughters had stalled at the second girl from the top. All eyes were trained on us. It looked like they'd been watching us this whole time. Even now, their heads volleyed side to side during the exchange watching with rapt attention as we openly and comically plotted our escape.

A deep bellied laugh ripped through the room. It was Thor. He left Ran's side, turning his back on her daughters as he did so. The big, hulking thunder god came toward me. "I choose this one."

Ran frowned in confusion. She squinted at me, as though trying to determine if I was one of hers. It was likely the blonde hair that gave me away.

"Oh, mighty Thor," Ran laughed, "that is not one

of mine. That I could birth something so pale with such a garish mop of hair."

Any fear of being caught fled from my body as I reached up to touch my hair. I may not have visited a salon in a few weeks, and I'd just been through a shipwreck, but my hair sure as hell wasn't garish or a mop.

Thor's golden gaze swept over my body like a heavy caress. He didn't spend a lot of time on my womanly bits. He focused on and held fast to that so-called garish mop. The light in his eyes flashed pure desire. I felt the resulting roll of thunder deep in my core.

"She is now mine," he said, his booming voice was a quiet storm. His tone brooked no argument, no discussion, no leeway.

"Well, of course," said Ran. "If you so desire it as a gift—"

"I desire her as my bride," Thor corrected.

"But she's a human," Ran protested.

Thor sniffed at my hair. His nose coming within an inch of my temple. I have no idea why I didn't raise my sword or my fist or even my voice against the invasion of my personal space. But I didn't.

"I don't know what she is," Thor said when he

pulled away from me. "But she is most definitely not human. Are you?"

I didn't answer. My mouth wouldn't work as I watched the lightning strikes in his eyes.

"It's you," Thor said quietly. His voice only loud enough for me to hear.

"Me?" I managed.

"From my dreams. Hair of spun gold that rivals the sun. Eyes like the sea right before a storm. All that's missing is the sword at your hip."

I gripped my satchel. He caught the movement and smiled. His eyes flashed at me again, like he knew what I hid at my side.

"It is you. My fair, Sif. You are meant to be my wife."

"Loren?" said a voice from far away, but I couldn't focus on it. My entire world was focused on this deity before me.

I should've been scared. Not that there was a god in my face determined to have me. Been there, done that.

He'd said the M word to me. *Marriage* was a threat in my mind; fighting words. But the way he said it, the way he proclaimed it, it kinda turned me on. No one had ever asked me to marry them. It was worth considering, if only for a second.

They say the odds of being struck by lightning in a single lifetime are slim, something like one in three thousand. Obviously, the odds of being struck twice were slim to none. But here I stood with lightning flashing before me with each blink of his eyes.

"Loren!"

I blinked my eyes after that last flash. I turned my attention to the guys. They didn't appear to be in awe of my luck at surviving a lightning storm. No one looked even slightly impressed; not the guys, or the sea gods, or their mermaid daughters. Well, Bara grinned with amusement as she regarded Thor and me.

"Is that your name?" said Thor. "Loren? It suits you."

I grinned at the compliment. My flirting instincts finally kicking in. I might've flipped my hair over my shoulder in Ran's direction.

"Loren!" Geraint, Gawain, and Tres all shouted in unison.

I winced at the combined strength of their voices. "Sorry about this," I said to Thor.

The adoration didn't leave his face as I dashed around him. I dove for his hammer. The weapon was within my grasp before anyone realized what was going on.

The tool was heavy, but I managed to lift it. I wondered if that meant I was now Queen of Asgard. Calling on every comic book I ever read, I wound the hammer around my head, swinging it like a majorette swinging a baton. Then I bent down and smashed the hammer into the ground.

A lightning bolt cracked through the room. The force of it rustled the net from the ground, giving my guys an opening. It knocked everyone else off their feet. Well, everyone except me and Thor.

Thor stood tall and proud. He didn't come after me for handling his tool. His hands came to rest on his hips as he let out another of those great belly laughs.

With all the gods and godlings distracted, I made my way to the guys. Well, my body did. My hand, the one wrapped around the hammer, didn't budge and I was jerked back toward the weapon. My hand still wrapped around the hammer's handle, I was yanked up and away.

The head of the hammer landed right smack dab into Thor's open palm. His free hand came around my body. He didn't free the hammer from my grasp. Instead, he pressed me into him, as though I were a nail and he was the board I was meant to be driven into.

"Marry me," he said.

There was a touch of crazy in his eyes. I noticed it because it was the same hue I'd seen a few times when I looked in the mirror.

"I have met my match," said Thor.

"You have no idea," said a deep voice that rivaled Thor's.

Tres's words shook me from my stupor. The crack of Tres's fist across Thor's jaw shook me out of the god's arms. At the shock, Thor let go of his hammer and me.

Tres caught me in his embrace. He wrapped his arms around me and, with the hammer still clutched in my hands, he raced out of the hall alongside Geraint and Gawain. I couldn't resist looking over Tres's shoulder to see what the mighty thunder god would do.

Thor licked at the cut on his lip. Then he picked up his feet and charged toward us. Fast as lightning.

"We need to get out of here," Tres said, taking the hammer from my hands. "How does this thing work? How do we get to Niflheim?"

"It's not the right hammer," I said.

"It's a hammer of a god," Tres insisted.

"It's Thor's hammer. It calls lightening. We need Odin's hammer to travel between the realms."

Tres's pace slowed as we came to the end of the hall. There was no place left to run. When we turned back to the other direction, we saw the hall filled with the broad body of the god of lightning. Coming up behind him were Ran, Aegir, and their jilted daughters. We were well and trapped.

My heart pounded in my chest as I tried to think. Something cold bounced on my chest. I looked down to see the necklace Gwin had given me. I wrapped my hand around it, feeling the pull of the magic encapsulated inside.

If I used the charm, our cover would be blown. If I didn't, we were likely to get blown to bits. Well, the guys would. I was more likely to be marched down an aisle by a handsome, virile, slightly crazy god.

With that thought, I yanked the chain from around my neck and began a chant. The hall filled with the energy of the ley line. The gods stopped moving and stared in horror.

"A daughter of Eva," screeched Ran. "A filthy witch in my house."

We didn't get to hear any more insults. A doorway of energy opened up in the wall. The four of us raced inside.

As the doorway shut, I saw a ginger head fill the

hole. Thor's gaze caught mine. Another flash of lightning struck, and I knew that this particular storm would be returning to my life at some point in the future.

13

We were traveling inter-dimensionally through a wormhole that bent space and time. That much was evident by the molecules separating from their groups and particles splitting apart to sever protons from electrons. This was an energy path, but it was not a ley line.

I didn't feel recharged falling through the multi-colored waves of light. The surge of frothing particles burned my skin. It gnawed at my bones. I felt it stripping my magic away.

It kicked and punched and scratched. I was certain I'd be bleeding when I came through the other side. If, miraculously, I came through the other side.

And it was cold. So cold, even though it flashed those five colors seen in the form of an arc after a rainstorm. I knew what this was, what we were traveling inside of. It could only be the Bifrost; the burning rainbow bridge that connected the nine realms of the Norse gods.

It left me to wonder, if we were traveling from one realm of the gods to another, why couldn't we simply use the Bifrost to travel to the core of the earth? In answer, the rainbow gave me a hard shake that left me dry heaving. I tried to pry my eyes open wider, but the light hurt, and I had to squeeze them shut.

Strong arms came around me. I knew they were Tres's arms without opening my eyes. Not that I would've been able to see anything except a prism of technicolor. But because I already knew what it felt like to be held in his arms.

I knew his heat. I knew his scent. I knew the salty, sweet taste of him. I could make out all those things even in this nothingness of the cold, glaring light of the Bifrost. All with my eyes closed.

I reached out, and I clung to him. That same sense of security from when we were being tossed about on his sinking yacht came over me again, and

I knew, that no matter where we ended up, everything was perfect in this moment.

I tried opening my eyes again. I had the greatest desire to look at him, to see what was in his eyes. Forcing my eyes open, I tilted my head. There was no emotion in his eyes. His eyes were pure light like his pupils had burned away and left behind a window to his soul, a soul of a nascent sun.

I had to be hallucinating. I closed my eyes again and tried to make sense of it all. But trying to arrange thoughts with all this energy pounding at me was the most difficult thing I'd ever done.

The journey through might've taken moments, it might've taken days. I had no idea? But, finally, we landed.

The impact into the other side knocked me out of Tres's embrace. It was like crashing in a car going at high speeds and neither of us was wearing seatbelts. Nothing could've kept us together after that blow.

I ached everywhere. My brain smooshed into the front of my skull. All my senses were jumbled. My nose was ringing. My ears were running. My eyes chattered.

I reached out for purchase, hoping to find a

handful of male flesh. Instead, I got a handful of grass and dirt.

I was alone. Tres was nowhere in sight. Had I imagined him holding me?

I was able to open my eyes without blaring pain now. There was no rainbow bridge in sight. I looked up to find myself in a glade of some sort. It glowed with a soft, yellow light. Looking up, I saw that I sat beneath the branches of a massive tree. It reminded me of a Bonsai with its angular, awning shape. Amidst the leaves were golden fruit.

The smell that wafted down from them was what I imagined heaven to be. My stomach didn't grumble with hunger. But something was salivating inside me, something deep in the core of my being where my magic sat.

I came to my knees and heard a gasp of pain. I whipped my head around, my eyes frantically searching. But I saw nothing. No one. Just a rolling plane of plants with huge bulbous heads.

There was a whooshing sound as the bulbs closed their petals. From my peripheral vision, I saw the petals peek open when my gaze wasn't directly on them. I scooted to my knees, looking around when I heard the screech of pain again.

"Ouch, you're on my head, you foul ape."

I looked down at the ground for the owner of the childlike voice. Leaves unfurled and stamen eyes peered back at me. I hopped out of the way. The plant's leaves trembled as it held a crumpled petal out.

"Leave me be or I'll tell my ovules on you."

"Oh, my god," I breathed. "I am so sorry. I didn't see you. Please let me help. What can I do?"

The plant swiped at my outreached hand. It tore into my skin with thorns, drawing blood. Rising on sturdy leg-like roots, the plant being took off running in the field, likely to tell its ovules on me.

I heard another rumble behind me. This wasn't a pained sound. It was laughter.

I hopped up, looking down for another stamen-eyed plant person. But there was only grass everywhere and small flowers. I hopped around like an idiot, certain I was murdering plant babies every time my foot touched down.

The laughing increased until, finally, I looked up and sought it out. The source of the laughter wasn't on the ground. It was up on a branch of the majestic tree.

A raven-haired man sat on a branch up in the tree. His back lounged against the tree's trunk. With a casual shove of his shoulder, he pushed off the limb. He was at least twelve feet in the air, but he landed easily on his feet with a quiet thud.

He'd stopped laughing and was looking at me with keen interest. He was handsome, in that way when men knew the power of their looks. He wore leather pants slung low on his hips. His dark shirt hung open exposing his defined chest.

He looked like the kind of man that was up to no good. He looked at me like he was expecting me to aim my boobs in his direction and flip my hair over my shoulder. He had villain written all over his high cheekbones and aquiline nose.

He was exactly my type of guy.

For the first time in my life, I didn't use my boobs as weapons against mankind. Instead, I reached instinctively for my sword stuffed inside the satchel slung over my hip.

The blackguard ignored my blade and swaggered toward me with purpose, coming forward until that bare sliver of chest caught the tip of my sword. It pricked his skin. Instead of red blood, a twinkle of light shone through where his skin broke.

"What are you?" he said once he'd stopped walking.

I could've asked him the same thing. Now that he was closer, I could see he was no mere man. He was easily over seven feet tall, but not broad like the thunder god. He was lanky, but there was a grace about his slightness. His hair was darker than night, but his eyes were clear and bright, positively sparkling with cunning.

He leaned in, ignoring the sword piercing his flesh. He sniffed at the air around my hair, just as Thor had done. Then he stuck out his tongue. I leaned back, but he didn't come any closer. He only tasted the air I'd just vacated.

"You're a daughter of Eva," he said, his eyes twinkling impossibly brighter. His grin spread wider than the joker's on a playing card.

"I don't know what that means?" I kind of had an inkling, though.

Eva, was the Germanic name of the first woman; Eve, the fabled mother of humanity. I feigned ignorance because playing dumb was the only defense I could think of with this being who was made of light pulled tight over living flesh.

"You shouldn't be here, daughter of Eva," he grinned conspiratorially. His voice was as low as a hiss. "Come to steal another apple?"

I looked up at the tree with the golden fruit. They didn't look like apples, not exactly. They looked more like pomegranates.

Myths and fables and stories collided in my head and tried to rearrange themselves into a cohesive tale. The Biblical Eve and the apple. The Norse tale of Yggdrasil, the world tree that connected all nine of the realms. The devilish serpent in the Garden of Eden. The trickster god of Nordic folklore.

"Loki?"

He grinned. Then he bowed, my blade scrapped a line up his chest as he did so. "At your service."

I retracted my blade but took another step back from him. Loki was known for his mischief, but he wasn't a killer. It was my wits that were in danger here, not my life. That is, if I was remembering these tales correctly.

"You're a witch," he surmised.

Crap. There went my cover.

"I can smell the sweetness on you." He came close and took another whiff.

"The sweetness?"

He nodded to the tree. "Your ancestor, a woman named Eva, stole the fruit of Yggdrasil. With its magic in her human blood, she attained many of the gifts of the gods. The sap of the fruit is seeping out of your pores. And yet you've come back for more? Are you a glutton?"

"I'm not here for the fruit." Though it was a

struggle to keep my eyes off the plump produce and my hands from reaching out for it. The desire to steal one of the golden orbs away was potent.

"Then what are you here for?" asked Loki.

My cover was already blown. He knew I was a witch, and there was no denying it. But if I told him the truth about my mission, he would likely try to find a way to trick me into doing his bidding. Still, I'd pit my mischievous nature against this imp any day.

"I'm here for Odin's hammer," I said.

Loki didn't look surprised. He only smiled. "Would you like my help?"

"What do you want in return?"

"I'll get you the All Father's hammer, for ... your head."

Right. I had forgotten. Decapitation was a favorite bargaining chip with the Norse gods. "Wait, do you mean that in a sexual way?"

Loki's grin spread so wide, the corners of his lips nearly touched the corners of his eyes.

"Because I'm not giving you either," I confirmed before he got too happy.

Loki pouted, the frown completely insincere. "Then I'm not helping you to get to Asgard."

"Isn't this Asgard?" I looked around at the wide fields filled with walking, talking plants.

"No. This is Alfheim. The realm of the fae."

Definitely not where I wanted to be. The fae knew who I was after I'd won their version of gladiator games in Rome a few weeks ago. Ran and Aegir might not come this way anytime soon, but if a fairy who'd come to the Colosseum saw me here it would definitely break the treaty.

Loki's gaze burned bright with fireworks as he watched my deliberation. Before I could think of a brilliant put down, an arrow shot between our bodies, causing us both to take giant leaps back.

The arrow had come from above. Up into the colorful sky there were dragons. It wasn't my first time seeing one of the magnificent beasts. One had been the opening act in Gyges's games in the Colosseum.

The flying dragons weren't the most shocking sight. Nor was the fact that there was more than one dragon. There were three, and atop each dragon's back were women dressed in armor with bows, arrows, swords, and shields in their hands.

"Great," said Loki. "Just what this day needed; Valkyrie."

14

The screams of ravens filled the sky. Even though there was not a black bird in sight. In Norse mythology, Valkyrie were known to take the shapes of crows and ravens. These women riding on the backs of dragons were not birdlike at all.

They did not have small heads perched on little bodies. They did not have round, feathered bodies. Nor were their toes skinny and three-pronged.

They were warriors. Tall, sleek Amazons of the sky. Curvaceous nymphs out of water. Sirens with long, lush tresses that sailed on the winds. Even from this distance, I could see that their eyes glowed golden bright.

The Valkyrie were also known as corpse

goddesses. They came to the battlefields of the fallen and chose amongst the slain warriors. The chosen they carted off to Valhalla. There, the dead warriors sat at the table of Odin, biding their time, preparing for the final battle yet to come.

Over the backs of the dragons, I saw bodies. Unmoving, male bodies. I knew they were males by the large boots they wore. I was too far to see any more of them. I didn't think I wanted to, not if they were what was left of a bloody battle.

In choreographed unison that race car drivers would drool over, the three women landed their dragons one next to the other. With a flap of their large, bat-like wings, the mighty beasts shook the ground. They folded their right wings, leaving their left outstretched. Each of the three Valkyries leaped down to the ground from those wings.

"Release the maiden," said one of the flying warrior women.

Her skin was a few shades darker than mine. Long, dark braids hung from the crown of her head and over pointy, elf-like ears. Like the others, she was dressed in battle armor with pale blue breastplates and golden epaulets. Her boots were white leather with a sturdy black seam.

They were seriously stylish. Not for the first time,

I wished that the Knights of the Roundtable would coordinate our wardrobe.

Loki held up his hands. Not like a criminal caught red-handed. More like a magician forced to reveal his best trick. "Do you see anything in my hands, Bryn?"

Undaunted, Bryn lifted a leather baton as she advanced on the trickster god. The cross looked like a hilt. A second later, the eighties fanatic in me bounced on her toes with glee as Bryn pressed some button and the sword flamed up.

It wasn't exactly the strobe lighting of a lightsaber. There were no waning light trails from CG effects or whooshing sound effects. Her flaming sword was pure electrical energy that roared like a fire.

Beside me, Loki sighed. He reached behind his back and pulled out a leather hilt of his own. With a flick of his wrist, his saber ignited. His flame was red to Bryn's ice-blue flame. Part of me wanted to watch this battle royale go down, but another part didn't want any blood on my hands.

"He's not holding me captive," I said.

The two light-wielding warriors ignored me. They instead focused their attention on ramming one another with their swords. The other two

Valkyrie approached me, crunching over the grass in their booted heels. The one in front had her hands raised as though approaching a lost child.

"You poor, helpless thing." Her skin was the color of Jasper stone, somewhere between an earthy orange and chocolate brown. Lush, red hair flowed in waves down her back. "I'm Hilda, and this is my sister, Siggy."

Siggy wiggled her fingers in greeting. Unlike her sister, Siggy had the deepest, even tan I'd ever seen. It was one shade away from being called golden. In sharp contrast, her hair was paler than snow.

I opened my mouth to introduce myself, but Hilda gave me a little shake which rattled my brain.

"You are in shock," she enunciated slowly, eyes wide as she came nose to nose with me. "You were stolen from your rightful place, likely carried off by a male. But we are here to free you from your unwanted confinement. You just catch your breath, little dear. We have saved the day."

She patted me on my head, like I was some frightened kitten. I was so dumbfounded by her monologue that I let her. I'd been mansplained to more times than I'd liked to count. This was the first time I'd had something chick-terpreted to me.

I couldn't say anything. Not if I wanted to keep

my cover as a witch in a place where I wasn't supposed to be. It chaffed, but I hunched my shoulders and tried to look submissive and afraid.

"Thank the gods you're here," I said in a breathy voice.

Loki delivered a blow to Bryn and then turned to glare at me. His narrowed eyes called me a liar and a fake. I held my tongue, holding my breath hoping Bryn's fist might connect with his smug face and keep his mouth shut.

Unfortunately, he ducked at the last second.

"Back up, Bryn," Loki said. "Or I'll tell your father."

"He's not around." Bryn did not stop her advance. She threw punch after kick after parry.

"When is he ever?" grumbled Loki as he dodged and ducked her strikes. "You lot run roughshod all over Asgard. But I tell you, the maiden is not under my hold. We were only talking."

"That's what they all say," said Siggy. "And then, the next thing you know, your armor is off and they're attacking what's beneath your breastplates."

"Really, Siggy." Hilda wrinkled her nose. "No one wants to hear about your distasteful carnal exploits."

Siggy lifted an indulgent eyebrow that screamed *Oh, yes they do.* But she held her tongue. With her sister seemingly chastised, Hilda turned her ire back on the sole male on the scene.

"You should be ashamed of yourself, Loki," said Hilda. "Picking on a defenseless sprout."

I was starting not to like this chick's tone. It was incredibly condescending. Even a bit patronizing, which was jarring for someone with breasts. Was there such a thing as matronizing?

"He does this all the time." Siggy leaned in to tell me. At least her tone was sympathetic and not lofty. "Loki tries to lure unsuspecting fairies into his lair to have his dirty, sweaty, lust-filled way with them."

Siggy's chest heaved as she listed her adjectives. My mind caught on the first part of her statement. Fairies? They thought I was a fairy?

"Bryn and Loki do this all the time." Hilda crossed her arms over her breastplate, huffing with impatience. "Fight with each other. You'd think there was some great romance."

I was a trained swordswoman. It was clear to see that both of the combatants were also well-versed in the art. It was even more clear, at least to me, that they were sparring as though they were in class and not fighting to draw blood. They twirled and flipped and did elaborate moves that were only done during competitions when a contender was trying to score performance points. Not the brutal moves required for real-life battle.

"You mean to tell me there's not a romance?" I asked.

Hilda wrinkled her nose. "Oh, no. Valkyrie don't have base instincts like humans. Except, maybe Siggy. And a few other of my sisters. But I happen to know Siggy was dropped on the head after her birth."

Out of everything that had happened to me over the past couple of weeks, this notion rocked me back on my heels. Grown women who were virgins. "I take it you never ... ?"

"Never what?" asked Hilda.

"She's talking about sexual intercourse," said Siggy.

Hilda looked disgusted. Like I'd just suggested strangling a kitten. Siggy waggled her eyebrows, grinning at the notion. Bryn thrust her sword at Loki, grunting with the effort.

"What would a fairy know about such things as the goings on between human men and women?" Hilda peered at me. "Are you newly sprouted? You don't have much coloring yet. And your ears are rounded."

"She's not a fairy," said Loki. He and Bryn were

locked in a clinch. Each was breathing heavily as their bodies pressed into one another. "She's a—"

Before he could get out my true nature, I interjected. "He's right. I'm not. I'm a human."

Bryn's gaze turned to me. Her guard dropped and the clench broke. She left herself wide open for Loki's attack. But now that she wasn't fighting anymore, Loki's hard gaze fell.

He rolled his eyes, withdrew his sword, and took off. But not before he winked at me. Then he turned his face up and looked to the sky. In the blink of an eye, his skin burned off. Like a piece of dust caught in a match's flame. He was nothing but light. He took off into the sky like a shooting star.

"A human woman?" said Bryn. "In Alfheim?"

Bryn looked from me to the tree. I followed her gaze. When I turned back to face the Valkyrie, they'd each drawn their swords of light and aimed them at me.

15

———

"Here to steal some fruit again?" asked Bryn.

It always came back to thievery. I'd never actually stolen anything from someone. Anything I'd ever taken was from someone who was dead. I'd taken things out of museums, out of tombs, but never out of anyone's actual hand. I had some morals.

Bryn finally noticed that Loki had slipped through her fingers. She looked up at the sky and screamed, or rather screeched, as his body dissipated into the clouds.

"Oh, let him go," said Siggy. "You two can poke each other with swords another day."

Bryn turned glaring eyes back on me like it had been my fault that she'd dropped her guard. "No human woman has breached this realm for three thousand years. How did you get here?"

"I ..." I figured I'd start at the beginning. "It was a shipwreck. Over the Bermuda Triangle."

The Valkyrie lowered their swords. Well, Siggy and Hilda did. Bryn still pointed hers at my left boob.

"Ran and Aegir," said Siggy.

"They must have sent her to us," said Hilda.

"They've never sent a female before," said Siggy. "What would we do with one?"

"I don't know?" Hilda frowned at me in consternation. "They don't have the strength we require that human men do."

It had to be the feminist in me that ignored self-preservation and reared her head to tell these women just how wrong they were characterizing me, and my entire species' gender. "They didn't *send* me. I *escaped*."

There was a pregnant pause, swollen with disbelief. Bryn burst out laughing. Siggy looked at me with an amused sort of pity. Hilda reached out and patted me on the head again. I dodged her hand before it could land.

"Bryn, lower your sword," said Hilda. "Can't you see she's just a lost, defenseless, little human woman? She's frightened to death. Look at her shaking."

Oh, I was shaking all right. With rage. There was nothing I wanted more than to test my magical blade against their light ones. But that would definitely confirm that I was a witch or at least a knight. And I already saw how that reaction played out.

So, even though my panties were bunched into a tightwad up my ass, I allowed the tremors that ran through my body to be mistaken for fear.

"We must show her compassion," Hilda was saying. "She's likely never seen women such as us in her short life. Warriors with the strength of body and spirit that no man could ever hope to test."

Had these Valkyrie never been to the human world? In any century? In any culture?

Not every woman on earth carried a weapon. None of them rode a dragon. Some weighed less than the armor these three carried on their backs. But human women were filled with cunning, craftiness, and an intelligence that kept the world spinning while men were busy exploring what was between their legs. If Valkyrie didn't recognize now, they would by the time I left this place.

"We're Valkyrie." Hilda smiled down at me like a first-grade teacher explaining why we didn't eat the crayons. "Daughters of the first god, Eden, and the All-Father, Odin."

"Yeah." I held out my hand. "Loren."

Hilda looked at my proffered hand. Her eyes brightened in response. "This is a human ritual. I've seen the males in Valhalla practice it. Wait, let me see if I can get it right."

Hilda lifted her hand, opened her palm, and spit in it. Then she looked up, eyes gleaming, and held out her frothy offering to me.

I recoiled, shaking my head. "That's really a guy thing. And, really, a young boy who doesn't care about hygiene thing."

Hilda lowered her hand with a frown. "How do women greet each other in the human world?"

"Um? Hugs. Double air kisses. They might say, *What's up, bitch.*"

Hilda gripped me in an awkward hug—note she hadn't wiped the spit from her palm—pursed her lips loudly in the air in front of my face, and then said, "What's up, bitch."

"Yeah. That's pretty good." I shrugged my shoulder to get out of her hold. The wet spot on my shoulder cap hadn't delayed her hand from releasing me.

"I like it," said Siggy. "Hey, Bryn. What's up, bitch."

"Whatever, bitch." Bryn turned around and headed back toward her dragon. "I want to get home with our bounty. We need this haul to feed the flames."

"Bounty?" I asked.

"Oh, yes," said Hilda. "We collect warriors from the battlefield."

"These days, it appears it's mostly the human infantry that die frequently," said Siggy. "The human leaders all seem to isolate themselves in glass towers and let the masses fight their battles for them, which leaves us with slim pickings."

"You see," said Hilda, "only the strongest of earth's spoils are of interest to us. We were presented with a fruitful harvest today. Come see what came across the Bifrost just now."

I followed them to the resting dragons. They had a point about military leaders. Hundreds of soldiers died each year from war, often more. But they were foot soldiers and not the men (or women) with stars and stripes on their shoulders.

"It's easy to believe that Ran and Aegir could've let a human woman slip into the Bifrost," said Siggy. "They've been preoccupied trying to marry one of their guppies off to Thor."

Hilda had been walking along proudly like a

soldier in a victory parade. But at the mention of Thor's name, she tripped. It took her only a second to right herself and regain her stride.

"Oh?" Hilda said. Her voice did not reach the level of carefree that I think she intended. She sent a furtive glance my way. "Did you happen to see Thor?"

"Big guy?" I asked. "Red hair? Loud hammer?"

"That would be him." Hilda chewed at her lip a moment. "Which daughter did he choose to wife?"

"He didn't choose any of them." Not a lie. He had barely glanced at the mermaids. But neither was I going to tell Hilda the full truth. It definitely didn't seem smart to unveil that I'd been his choice while she was hard at work feigning disinterest.

I was trying to decide what tale to spin that would best get me out of their hair and back on the road to finding the guys, when I heard a male groan.

Ask and ye shall receive because there they were. Strapped to the hides of the dragons with rope, the men with the big boots, were none other than Geraint, Gawain, and Tres. This journey was becoming incredibly fetishized.

"Those are my friends," I said.

"Those men are the spoils of war," said Bryn.

"The only way a human male can get to this realm is to die on the battlefield."

"Yeah, well, they're not dead," I insisted.

"Of course they are," said Bryn.

"Actually, Bryn," said Siggy. "They're waking."

Gawain was the first to stir. He tried to move his torso, but whatever had him tethered held him firm. Beside him were Geraint and Tres, still knocked out, but in the same predicament.

Wain lifted his head and saw me. "Did we get captured? Again? This is so embarrassing."

"How's this possible?" said Bryn. "No mortal man can travel the Bifrost while the breath of life is still within him."

"Well, they're breathing," said Siggy.

"Maybe they're not mortal men?" said Hilda.

"What other kinds of men are there?" asked Bryn.

Two of the men in question, Wain and Gerry, cracked muscles and tendons as they tried to rise. I felt the air change around the Valkyrie. Something hot entered the atmosphere, making me want to press my thighs together. I wondered if they'd ever seen a live human man before? Their eyes flashed with interest. Even Hilda's.

"Listen," I said, "since they're not dead, and Valkyrie choose from the slain warriors, can you just give them back to me. We'll find our way out of this realm and not bother you all again."

"This is a strange anomaly," said Hilda, ignoring me. "Perhaps something is wrong with the Bifrost?"

Finally, Tres came back to consciousness. His big body shook with a start. The material he was tethered with held firm, but only for a second. With a great shudder and a mighty roar, Tres broke the bindings. His chest heaved as he gulped down lungfuls of air.

"That's no mortal," said Bryn.

"I can explain," I began.

Once he had enough air in his lungs, Tres opened his eyes and looked around. He found me first, concern etched in his gaze. But I couldn't look at him. I had to shield myself from his glare. He wasn't angry at me. His eyes flashed that same light that they had in the Bifrost.

"Could it be?" breathed Hilda.

"An Ishim?" said Bryn.

Hilda turned to me with a smile. "Now it makes sense how you withstood the Bifrost. Why didn't you just tell us you belonged to an Ishim?"

16

Once the Valkyrie learned that Tres was an Ishim, a child of a god and a human, their attitudes completely changed. They released the binds around Geraint and Gawain and placed us all astride the backs of the dragons. Tres rode at my back. The dragon's hide was spacious and secure, but he pulled my back against his front regardless. I didn't protest.

The dragons took off, and commercial air travel, even by private jet, was forever ruined now that I flew Valkyrie Airways. To feel the sun on my skin and the wind in my hair as the world fell away. The pulsing heat of the dragon, the feel of the smooth scales, the sound of their wings as they soared. It was all etched into my brain, and I knew I'd dream this reality for always.

We left the fae realm as the sun set over the lush landscape. The plant-shaped people burrowed into the ground with their energy source tucking into the horizon. The pastel structures of the fae world, Alfheim, gave way to the silver and gold domed ziggurats of Muspelheim.

Somehow, there were three suns in this sky. Down there, lived beings of fire, Hilda told me. I would've thought that that was where dragons were born. Instead, I saw ships of metal winging around the vast realm. Furnaces burned, lighting the city. Fire escaped the exhausts of the ships' hindquarters.

It was clear when we crossed the boundary into Asgard. The energy changed. The realm looked like one great castle that went on like a mountain range. Spires rose and fell across the land but none so high as the one we aimed for.

"Is this Valhalla?" I asked as the dragon touched down without a single bounce.

"No," said Hilda. "It's Grimnir Hall. You can reach Valhalla from within. You can reach any of the five hundred halls from here. But no need to worry. The doors of Valhalla are sealed shut. They won't get out."

"They?" I asked. "Who?"

Hilda didn't answer. She walked into the hall and I followed. A cacophony of high-pitched, birdlike calls rose from within. Husky feminine laughter and un-hushed chatter greeted my ears from the doorway.

Rows and rows of tables spread out before me. Atop each surface was dish upon dish of savory smelling food. Pitchers of brown-golden liquid flowed in mugs and down chins and chests. It had all the hallmarks of a bar, but there wasn't a single male in sight. There were only Valkyrie in every corner of the dining hall.

The moment I crossed the threshold, a mug was shoved into my hand and all cares got lost in the sweetness of the honey wine. I rolled the fermented honey water around my tongue. Sloshing it from side to side to discern its structure. The alcoholic beverage was perfectly balanced, so I let it slide down my throat. Then I wrapped my hand around the mug of mead and tossed back what was left of the contents.

The Valkyrie around me all cheered. They raised their swords, shook their spears and bows, and flashed their golden eyes at me like cats at midnight.

In return, I saluted the Valkyrie like a soldier returned from war.

I'd never been in favor of an all-girls school, but the excess estrogen flowing through the eating hall awakened something in me; camaraderie, sisterhood. Were our periods synching? Did Valkyrie even have menstrual cycles?

"It's been a long time since an Ishim visited Asgard," said Hilda from her place beside me at our table. "Did my mother send you?"

"Your mother?" I asked.

"Yes," said Bryn. "Our mother. Eden. Being of light. The first being. You apes call her God. Lives in Niflheim, I believe you call it heaven, even though it's not in the sky. It's down in the core of the earth where all life began."

The guys and I exchanged looks. Well, Wain caught my gaze. Gerry was too busy looking around at the fae women serving the beer and food. Unfortunately, there wasn't a purple fae princess in sight.

"We're on our way there," Tres said.

"It's six realms away," said Bryn. "In the opposite direction."

"I was curious about Asgard," he said, easily covering. "I was hoping to meet Odin."

"Our father is not at home," said Siggy. She

sidled up to him. I noted her breastplate was off and her boobs were spilling over her loose blouse.

"He's off on another of his quests for knowledge," said Hilda.

"He's been alive since the dawn of time," said Bryn. "What more does he need to know?"

"Where is he?" Tres directed the question to Hilda who was on the other side of the table from him.

Siggy leaned into him to answer. "Far, far away in another realm. We don't expect him back for at least another decade at the earliest."

"Ten years?" I said. "That doesn't sound like a business trip to me. It sounds like child abandonment and neglect."

Bryn glared at me. "Why does your pet think she can speak to her betters? Have you not trained her well?"

I opened my mouth to respond. Tres's gaze connected with mine. Actually, his focus was on my lips. I let out a gush of air, effectively silenced beneath the flash of heat.

"She's not my pet," Tres said.

"Is she your spawn?" said Bryn. "From your loins?"

"No." Tres chuckled lightly, picking up his mug. "She's not my daughter."

"Did you give her your seed?" asked Siggy. "Placed some in her vagina? Or in her mouth?"

Tres coughed and spluttered the sip he'd taken of the sweet mead.

"She can't be a simple human," said Bryn. "There's no reason a human woman could withstand the Bifrost without some type of enhancement. If not your seed, then some other Ishim male's?"

"Or a woman's," said Hilda. "I'm told that happens down in Midgard."

"She's not my lover," said Tres. He did not lift his gaze to mine that time. His fingers rubbed at the condensation melting down the side of the glass.

"What is she then?" asked Bryn.

Watching Tres, I grit my teeth. One kiss didn't make me his. Neither did the fact that he sought me out and held me in the Bifrost and the dragon ride here. It was just protection. He was my best friend's ex. That made us ... I wasn't sure what that made us?

"She's my ..." Tres began. He lifted his head and studied me. I narrowed my eyes at him waiting to see what word he'd use. "Friend."

The kiss of death. He'd just friend zoned me. The bastard.

"Maybe she stole your seed while you slept," said Bryn. "I've heard that happens too in Midgard."

I slammed my hand down on the table. Enough was enough. "That is the second time you've called me a thief today."

It was also the third time she'd insinuated that I was a slut. But I had to prioritize the insults.

All went silent at my outrage. The fae servants backed away from the tables. The Valkyrie leaned in. The men balled their fists but relaxed them as they looked around at the room filled with women.

"Loren," said Tres in a warning tone.

"That's right, Loren," said Bryn. "Heel. Do as your master says."

I was about to correct these misandrists on just who, more often than not, wore the pants amongst the human genders. I opened my mouth to respond, but something purple moved into my peripheral vision. Or rather, someone purple.

Geraint stiffened. His eyes darting around the space anew. Unfortunately, he still didn't find whom he wanted.

"What are you doing here, Gyges?" said Bryn. "You know my father isn't at home. No one here is interested in any of your games."

"I heard you had special guests." Gyges's cunning

eyes swept over the four of us, landing and holding on me.

This was not good. Gyges knew both me and Geraint. He knew what we were. He could blow our cover with a single word. Or worse, he could let the knights know about the memento I'd received from him and not told them about.

"It's been a long time ..." Gyges swung his gaze from me and onto Tres. "... since I've met an Ishim."

Tres looked the fairy up and down. It was clear from the quickness of the perusal that he found Gyges wanting. But the businessman kicked in and Tres offered his hand. Gyges wrinkled his nose but took Tres's offering lightly. As soon as his fingers were released, Gyges made a show of discretely wiping off his hand with a rose petal.

Gyges took a seat at the end of the table with a flourish of his coat tails. "I wonder if you might've seen something unique on your travels to our fair realm? I seemed to have misplaced my daughter."

Beside me, I felt Gerry's whole body come alive, like a wire sliced from a powerline and now sending sparks as it writhed on the asphalt. I put my hand on his knee, but it was solid as a rock.

"She's purple," Gyges continued. "Feminine, delicate. Have you seen her?"

"No," said Tres.

"They're on their way to Niflheim," said Hilda.

Tres, the only focused one of our little party, turned the conversation back to where we needed it to go. "If Odin isn't here, can anyone tell me the fastest way to Niflheim?"

"Can't you just shed your flesh and go?" asked Hilda.

"Shed my flesh?" asked Tres.

"Yes. You're an Ishim. Travel there in your true essence, your light."

Tres looked dumbfounded.

"Your father never taught you how to do that?"

"I've never met my father."

"Typical," said Bryn. "The gods are perpetually too busy for their offspring."

"My daddy never paid attention to me." Siggy pouted her lower lip and aimed it at Tres.

"I hear Ishim parents pluck them out of Niflheim and place into Midgard when they're just a century old," said Hilda. "It's positively cruel."

"Cruel as it may seem," said Tres, "I would like to get down there. Is there a way to do it with my flesh intact?"

"You're that desperate to see your father?" said Bryn.

"No." He looked down at the table. "There's a woman ..."

I turned away so I didn't have to see his expression of unrequited love for my best friend. I wish I could be farther away from him so that I didn't have to feel the heat of his skin to remind me of things that had transpired between us.

But Tres only finished with, "... she's important."

Nia was important. To both of us. And I had to keep that at the forefront of my mind.

"You've done all this, risked the wrath of Ran and Aegir, traveled the Bifrost, and now come seeking the advice of our father, for a woman?"

The Valkyrie, all two dozen present, stared at him, dumbfounded.

Tres nodded.

"There is a way we could help you without our father's aide," said Bryn. Something about the way she eyed Tres set me on edge. It wasn't carnal. It was carnivorous. "But it would come at a great cost."

"Bryn." Hilda's tone was a warning. "He's an Ishim. He's one of us."

"He's a male and an Ishim. You know what that kind of power could mean for us."

The sisters stared silently for a moment.

"Speaking of bright, shiny, powerful things ..." said Siggy.

Hilda's concern melted away. The rapid pounding of her heart reached me through the short space between our skin. I felt his heat before I lifted my head. The flames of his hair blinded me first, before his golden gaze locked on me.

Hilda quickly regained her composure and stood. "You honor us with your presence, great warrior."

She reached out her hand, but Thor moved past her on purposeful steps. He didn't glance at her at all. He made a beeline for me.

"There you are," he said, swooping me out of my seat.

Geraint and Gawain stood. Neither of them had weapons. But their strength caught the thunder god's attention.

"Are these your suitors?" Thor asked.

"No," said Geraint. "She's our brother."

Thor looked me over. I knew he felt my boobs and curves against his chest.

"Can you put me down, please?" I asked. Thor's hold was warm and strong, but I didn't need any more attention on me than I already had. "Everyone's staring and you're causing a bit of a scene."

"This is a joyous occasion," the golden god said, his voice booming. "I've found my Sif at last."

Hilda made a choked sound. "Your Sif?"

"Yes, Hilda." Thor looked down at her as though he were seeing her for the first time. "I told you when we were nascent. I had a dream of a woman with golden hair. That she would be the one I'd spend all of eternity with. And here she is."

watched Hilda's eyes glaze over in real time. Crap. I'd just made an enemy. Of a fierce, bloodthirsty Valkyrie.

"I didn't say I was going to marry him," I said.

"Why wouldn't you marry him?" asked Hilda.

Her voice was stilted, her features iced over to reveal as little of her emotions as possible. I knew that pose. I'd struck it myself with a certain Greek warrior in my past.

"He is the bravest, strongest warrior in all of the Nine Realms. Any woman would be honored to have him lay down his life for hers."

"Ah, Hildy," said Thor. "This is why you've always been my best friend."

Hilda winced. Yeah, welcome to the friend zone. Not so cute.

"Will you be the first to congratulate me on my impending nuptials?" Thor said.

Hilda's mouth worked like a fish out of water. "But she's a human."

"I thought so too," Thor laughed. "But she's actually a—"

I reached up and kissed him. It was the only way I could think to shut him up so quickly. It was also a mistake.

I'd been kissed more than my fair share in my short life. I'd been kissed well more often than not. The kiss I'd had with a certain Broody Billionaire not too long ago could easily rank as the top lip-lock to ever come knocking on my door. Thor's showing nearly knocked Tres down a notch. Almost.

It had to be the electricity within him. I felt a buzz humming through my blood. It wasn't the alcohol. Booze loosed my knees, it didn't make me press my thighs together, and right about now, a penny couldn't get through my knotted knees.

I heard throats clearing, a couple of catcalls, and a few gasps. I tried to pull away, but Thor would not let go. I managed to get my lips free, but not my body from his embrace.

"Can we go somewhere and talk?" I asked, my voice breathy as I tried to inhale air at the same time as exhale words.

"I know the perfect place," Thor said.

He didn't set my feet on the ground. He carried me bodily out of the hall.

Gerry and Wain made to follow. I lifted my hand to let them know I had this. Thankfully, they trusted me enough to believe me.

Tres didn't back down so quickly. His jaw ticked as the distance increased between us. Honestly, that made my belly feel warmer. I wasn't game-playing, I was saving us. But it did my feminine pride good to know that Tres had been ticked off after seeing another man sample the goods he'd zoned in on.

Once the door to the dining hall closed behind us, I wriggled in Thor's arms. "Put me down."

"You might run off again," he said. "I've already spent the day chasing after you."

I kneed him in his belly. He was lucky I aimed high and missed his groin. He doubled over with a grunt. No, that was laughter.

"Thank the gods my wife is a strong witch."

"Shhh." I tried to hush him. "You know about the treaty between Odin and people like me?"

Thor reached for my hair. I slapped his hand

away, but it didn't deter him. He captured one of my locks and twirled it around his long, thick, neatly kept fingers.

"You know what Odin's daughters will do if they find out what I am?"

"They would never," Thor insisted. "You're mine."

"I am not yours."

He frowned, but he didn't let my lock of hair go. Nor did he give me an inch of personal space.

"Where I come from, if you force a girl against her will it's not romantic. At least not without a safe word. Mine is *no*. I've been using it repeatedly."

"You don't wish to marry me?"

"I don't wish to marry anyone." I tripped over that last word.

All my life I felt pretty certain that I wasn't the marrying kind. But something changed recently. Maybe it was the shipwreck. Or maybe it was my journey through the Bifrost. Whatever it was, Thor heard that tiny catch in my voice, and he pounced on it.

I took a step back. Partly to get out of his reach, but also because I felt a pull. My feet felt drawn down the hall to a certain door.

Light burned bright beneath the simple wood door. Once I was in front of it, I reached out to put my hands on the door. Before I could make contact, Thor pulled my hands away.

"Don't go that way, my little witch," said Thor.

"I'm not yours," I said, but he ignored me. "What's through there?"

"That's the entrance to Valhalla."

"Valhalla? Where the Valkyrie take the dead warriors?"

Thor pressed my back to his front. With my head tucked beneath his chin, I felt him nod above my head.

"There are dead men in there?"

He didn't answer. He buried his nose in my hair.

"Why is it so warm?"

"Ah-ah. Don't touch."

Thor pulled my hand, which had been reaching for the handle, away.

"That door must not be opened," he said, pressing a kiss to each of my fingers.

"Why not?"

"Do not concern yourself with that." He turned me away. "Tell me how to win your hand, for I am certain of my feelings. Only you will be my bride."

I looked into his eyes. His bright, fire-fueled, crazy eyes. They were earnest. "I need Odin's hammer."

Thor threw back his head and laughed, that great belly laugh that sounded like crackling thunder. "My bride has a sense of humor. I will spend my days in passion and pleasure."

"I'm not marrying you."

"Why not?" He trailed a finger down my face. "Do you not find my form pleasing?"

"You're hot, and I think you know it."

"My temperature? It's not pleasing to you?"

"No—it. You're very pleasing to look at."

Thor grinned. "Do you think I cannot protect you? Ask anyone and you'll learn that the name of Thor strikes fear into the hearts of all kinds."

"Your reputation precedes you."

"I have riches. I will cover you in jewels and fine silk."

My tongue got tied then. I was a materialistic beast at heart. But I couldn't abandon Nia.

"I know you can feel the physical attraction between us," he continued.

Thor leaned his head down. My brain told me to back away from him, but that energy between us crackled, holding me in place like a magnet. And then, suddenly, the polarities shifted.

Thor jerked away from me. His arm raised as he aimed his hammer and released the weapon. It flew, mallet first, from his hand and arrowed toward a dark figure in the hall.

"Wait!" I cried.

The hammer halted. Less than an inch in front of Tres's heart. Tres wasn't looking at the hammer. He was looking at me and Thor. I felt the heat of his gaze like a caress even though another man held me in his arms.

Thor might've seen it too. His grip tightened on me, and his gaze narrowed. Tres didn't raise a foot to come to my rescue. He didn't extend a hand. He didn't say a word. He simply nodded his head and turned back into the hall.

"Now," said Thor. "If we have all those matters cleared up, will you be my bride?"

It took a moment for my gaze to leave the spot that Tres had vacated and focus back on Thor.

"You were meant for me," said Thor. "I saw you in a dream. I never dream of anything but the glory of battle. And then I saw you. It is meant to be."

"I don't believe in fate," I said. "Or fairytales."

"You're not fae. And it's not fate. It was a dream. Dreams are the visions of our deepest desires."

"By that logic, I should've dreamed of you too."

"You haven't?"

I didn't answer immediately. I'd had plenty of

dreams of a man sweeping me off my feet. What woman who read or watched Disney didn't.

"If I don't accept your proposal," I asked, "you'll rat me out that I'm a witch and broke the treaty?"

"I'll keep any secret you wish," he said.

"Why should I trust you?"

"Why would I lie? I want to make a life with you. Gods live long lives. Females have even longer memories."

"What you're feeling sounds like lust to me."

"That too," Thor grinned. "I have a mighty lust for you, Loren."

The way he said my name it sounded like Lure Rain. Like he was luring me in drop by drop.

"Now you're talking my language," I said. "But marriage? I'm not that kind of girl."

Thor frowned. "What kind of girl? The kind to be worshiped for her beauty, praised for her cunning, cherished for her loyalty? You're not that kind of girl?"

My tongue was knotted, but I unraveled the gnarled bits quickly. "You don't know me. I don't know you."

"We have an eternity to learn one another. I can provide for you, protect you, pleasure you. Tell me what you need."

The tangle returned.

"What are you afraid of?" Thor asked.

What was I afraid of? Because that was fear in my heart. "Nia. I have to save my friend. She's trapped in Niflheim."

"She's dead?" he asked.

"No. Well, yes. I'm not sure."

"She's Ishim? Half god, half human. If so, she's not dead."

"She still needs me," I insisted.

"How can I help? I'll do anything in my power."

"I need Odin's hammer to travel between the realms."

"That's not within my power."

"Can you get me to Niflheim any other way?"

"Just as you and your magical kind are not meant to return to this realm, my kind are not meant to return there. But you must know your friend cannot die. She will return to the surface someday, likely in a few centuries or millennia. Become my wife and you will live to see that day."

"Loren?" Geraint approached us from the direction of the dining hall. He spoke to me but his gaze was on Thor. "It's time to go."

"Go?" I said. "Go home? No. I'm not giving up."

"No need." Gawain materialized behind Geraint.

"Tres made a deal with the Valkyrie. They can go to the core of the earth and get Nia back."

That seemed all too simple.

"What kind of deal did he make?" I asked.

"He gave up his soul to the Valkyrie."

18

———

Tres stood outside the hall. He leaned his broad back against the structure of the great fort's wall and looked up at the sky. I still didn't understand how we saw the moon in this realm? I wondered if it was the same moon that my family back in Camelot slept under?

Tres wasn't alone. Bryn spoke to him in hushed tones. I couldn't hear her words, but the tone was sharp and commanding, like she was a general issuing orders to a private.

When she was done talking, she patted her hand on his chest in a proprietary manner. My hands flamed. Bryn must've smelled the smoke because she looked my way. Luckily, my hands were clenched and shoved behind my back. A smirk spread across

Bryn's admittedly pretty features. It was tempting to blow my cover now just to burn that look off her face.

My forced nonchalance must've worked. A second later, she turned on her booted heel and headed back into the hall. She said nothing as she passed me. She didn't need to. I wasn't exactly sure what kind of game was being played here, but her victory was clear. I felt a profound sense of loss as the great doors to the hall closed quietly behind her.

Tres and I were left alone in the dark. The night filled with unfamiliar sounds as creepy crawlers bumped about on more than four legs. There was a breeze, but not an airy one. It felt more like a wave of energy; aggressive and tenacious. Like one of those small lapdogs facing off against a breed three times its size. The pup couldn't do any damage, but it was irritating nonetheless.

Tres didn't turn to me as I approached him. His heat greeted me like the first dip of a pinky toe into a hot bubble bath, right before plunging all the way in. I wasn't going to take the plunge. That was the plan anyway.

And then that earthy scent of Frankincense wrapped around me and pulled me toward him until I was in line with his shoulder.

"What's this I hear about you surrendering?"

"It's the only way," he said. "I want Nia and Zane back. I don't want anyone else to have to suffer, not if I can help it. I've caused enough suffering in my life. The Valkyrie are allowed to travel between the realms, something about a custody agreement between their parents. They'll go to Niflheim and get Nia and Zane. They'll send you three back to Midgard, never learning what you truly are. The treaty will remain in place. Everyone gets what they want."

"That sounds way too easy. What's the catch?"

"I stay here," he said.

"You stay here ... and what?"

"It doesn't matter." His voice was soft and tired, completely at odds with the strong, virile man that he was.

"It matters to me."

His eyes were a shade lighter than the dark night. They pierced through me in the twilight. His gaze on me felt like standing under the noonday sun. There was no place to hide.

The full heat of his glare lingered a breath too long on my lips. I saw a spark there, but it was doused before it could get any oxygen to feed it. All too quickly, the light in his eyes dimmed and turned back to look out on the gloomy landscape.

"Tres? What happens to you?"

"I told you," he said. "I'll stay here."

"Where? In Valhalla? To be a part of Odin's dead army?"

He nodded.

"But you're not dead."

"I'm immortal. I won't die. It won't be the end of me. The deal is a stay for a few hundred years. I consider it a prison sentence for my crimes."

He wouldn't be dead, but I might be. Witches had long lives. I might live to a thousand, but I'd be old and wrinkly by then, my boobs pointing at my knees, my hair thin, or worse—gray. I shuddered to think that he might see me like that.

"What exactly will they do with you?" I asked.

"I'm not exactly sure."

"You'll be a boy toy."

Tres grinned, but there was no pleasure in it. "Yeah, I don't think it works like that with them."

"Percy called the Valkyrie carnivorous. Do you think they eat the men they capture?" I placed my hand on my stomach where the delicious meat I'd just ingested rested heavily. "Do you see any males around here?"

"They're all in the Hall of Valhalla."

"So a guys' weekend that lasts centuries?"

Tres shrugged. "Could be worse."

"I'm supposed to be the martyr," I said. "You're stealing my thunder."

"No, he's standing over there." Tres aimed his strong chin at Thor.

I turned to see the thunder god leaning against the open doorway, unabashed as he listened to our conversation.

"You could do worse," said Tres.

"You could do better."

"I don't deserve better."

"That's not true," I said. "You're a good man. You made beautiful things all over the world. Left the world a better place."

"I'm not the hero of this story, Loren. My motives are always selfish, except this time. I've hurt more innocent people than I care to remember. I betrayed my friends. Zane finally gave up on me."

"I thought he saved your life in that underground cave?"

"Because he's a good person," said Tres. "And that's what good people do. Even after you seduce their soulmate just because you want to know what love feels like."

"Did you find out?" I asked. "What love feels like."

Tres didn't answer that question. He closed his eyes and tilted his head up to the moonlight. I took a moment to take in his profile. Would this be the last time I'd ever see him?

"People change," I said.

"No, they don't." He shook his head, his brow heavy. "I've been alive long enough to know. You can make different decisions, but they're all choices. Instinct is who you are. Instincts don't change."

I reached into my satchel and handed him the figurine I'd rescued from the shipwreck. He smiled down at it, his eyes crinkling with sadness. He turned the figure over in his hand, rubbing his thumb over the face of the lion.

"Zane carved this for me in 2700 BC, when I was king of Sumer."

Why did all the men who insisted on friend zoning me end up being from royalty? Was there prince repellent in my deodorant? King-away in my lip gloss?

"I was a jerk of a king and a piss poor excuse for a man before he showed up. I didn't know how to be a friend. There was no one else like me in the world. Or so I thought. And then he turned up and punched me in the face. Knocked some sense into me. That was the first time I felt love."

I blinked up at him.

Tres grimaced in annoyance. "Not sexual. He punched me because he cared about what would happen to me. I mattered to him. But I couldn't escape my instincts. I always put myself first. When you love someone, you put them first. I'm doing that now. For both of them."

Tres looked down at me again. There was light in his eyes now. But that light was bleak.

"You're a good friend, Loren. Nia is lucky to have you."

"Even though I made out with a guy my best friend was kinda sorta dating?"

Tres shook his head. "I never had a chance with Nia. Not a real one. Zane knew it. It's why he's not pissed at her. He's pissed at me."

"So, we're both sluts?"

"I believe the male term would be whore."

I punched him in his shoulder. He feigned pain, but gave the farce away when he chuckled. His grin slid as he took me in. I held my breath as we stared at each other.

And there it was again; that wordless, soundless, motionless sensation. Everything around us stopped. I didn't feel the urge to kiss him or jump his bones. I just felt like holding still and staying forever in this moment.

That same feeling of security came over me. I wanted more of it. To give it as well as receive it.

"If you go with them," I said, "this will be the last time I see you."

"What? You'll miss my big boat and the car and the money?"

"No," I shook my head. "I never got to drive your car."

Tres laughed again. I did too. It was so easy with him. Effortless now that we got past that layer of suspicion of whether or not I was here for his money, and whether or not he'd hurt my friend. If we'd had more time, we could've been ... something.

Tres kicked off the wall and began a slow march toward the hall. "Tell them both that I love them."

Love? Them? Right. Nia and Zane.

I meant to confirm that I would pass those words along. The problem was I wanted some of my own.

"What about me? Any words for me?"

Tres looked over his shoulder. He turned around, but kept walking backward. He smiled as he regarded me. "Don't change. Follow your instincts."

19

My instincts told me to reach out and grab him before he got away. My instincts told me to run after him and hug tackle him to the ground. To at least snag one more kiss from him before he was forever out of my reach.

An electric blanket doused my instincts. Warm arms wrapped around me. A broad chest cradled my back. My head came to rest under a hairy chin.

"Was he your lover?"

Thor's voice slipped down from the crown of my head to curl my toes. The feel of him charged me, sending volts into each of my cells and making them light up like dueling neighbors in a battle over Christmas light decorations.

"It's none of your business," I said from within the hum of his embrace.

"It is entirely my business as you will be my wife soon."

I let out a slow and weighted sigh. It took every ounce of energy he'd given to me to step out of his embrace and lift a warning finger to him. "What kind of man are you? Did you not just see that my friend got taken into captivity by a bunch of bloodthirsty vigilantes?"

Thor reached out and captured a few strands of my hair, letting them slide through his fingers. "Bloodthirsty is a bit harsh. The Valkyrie don't actually consume the warriors they take to Valhalla. That's just a story the fae tell their sprouts at sunset."

"He's more than my friend." I'm not sure when that happened. Sometime between shoving him into Nia's irresolute arms and having a taste for myself.

Thor's jaw tensed. The confidence he'd displayed for the last twenty-four hours ebbed. His golden eyes darkened to amber.

"He's my family," I said. "No one messes with my family."

Thor studied me, rubbing the ends of the strands of my hair between his thumb and index finger. His eyes spoke volumes, but he held his tongue. No, that wasn't the look of someone holding their tongue, he was choosing his words.

"Is this the part where you tell me if I agree to marry you, you'll save Tres?"

"No."

Oh. That was disappointing. It would've been an option I'd consider, especially since it would've put me back in the martyrdom seat.

"If you agreed to share your life with me at the price of another man's soul then you would not be the woman of my dreams."

"Wait? So you'll help me get him back? Or you won't?"

"I could," Thor said. "But there is a cost, and I'm not certain you would like the toll."

"Try me."

"If I rip the Ishim from the Valkyries' grasp, you won't get your—what did you call it?—bestie back."

Crap. So this is what it would come down to? Tres's life for Nia's. Seriously? Just for one day, could life be fair to me?

"Loren?"

Geraint and Gawain stood in the opened doorway back into the main hall. "It's time to go home," said Gerry. "Hilda is ready to take us to the Bifrost and send us back to Midgard."

Thor stepped between me and my brother knights. "Loren is home. Her place is with me."

"You know what she is," said Wain. "You know she can't stay here."

"You know what I am," Thor said. "You know why I can't go to your realm. She'll live in my hall. No one need ever find out that she is a daughter of Eva."

With the door wide open, the three men began to argue about my future in hushed tones. They became radio static in the background as my attention focused beyond them. Bryn and Siggy walked with Tres down the long hallway. Siggy's eyes roamed him like he was a piece of meat, totally negating that carnivorous argument.

Tres caught my gaze upon him. He looked over and gave me a pointed nod. It said very loudly and very clearly, *farewell.*

I walked past Thor. I pushed past my brothers. "What are they going to do to him?"

"He's an Ishim," said Thor. "He'll be fine. I'm sure."

He didn't sound sure.

"You're not answering my question," I said.

"They're taking him towards the doors to Valhalla. The ones you said couldn't be opened."

"I said for you not to open them," said Thor. "Those doors can't be opened until the day of the final battle. There is another way in."

"And that's where they're taking Tres? To the secret entrance of the hall of dead human warriors?"

Again, Thor didn't answer me. One look at his face told me that he wanted to answer me. His jaw clamped hard enough that I heard his molars grinding. He didn't quite meet my gaze, looking instead at my ear or the hair that covered that side of my face.

I turned from him and back to Tres. It felt wrong, watching Tres being led away. Watching the women ogle his body. Well, they weren't exactly ogling his body. They looked through him.

I had to wonder did they see the man behind the facade? Tres wanted to be loved but didn't believe himself worthy. He wanted a family but didn't know how to reach out. He wanted to belong, but he didn't know how to fit his limbs in a family-sized shape.

That was me. I had been Tres just a short time ago. But I'd changed.

Sure, I still had the same impulses. But I made different choices every single day. I made those choices because the consequences, the repercussions to those I loved, were too high a price to pay.

I screwed up from time to time. Okay, a lot. But my family and friends never withdrew their support. They latched onto me, predicted my behavior, and tried to save me from myself.

Tres deserved that kind of love and support. He didn't deserve to suffer for a hundreds of years because he'd taken a chance, reached out for love, and his gamble had failed.

"I know that look," Gerry groaned.

That look he was seeing was me trusting my instincts.

I turned to look up at Thor. The golden god ran his thumb across his lower lip, his gaze never leaving me. The irony didn't escape me. Here was a man giving me the full court press, and my attention was on the man who'd literally just turned his back on me.

"Listen, Thor," I began. "I really appreciate—" I waved my hands between our two chests, "—all this. It's just that I'm still getting over a really bad break up, and I almost got into something that probably would've wound up hurting me even more so ..."

This was not the direction this conversation was

meant to go. I gave myself a shake. Turning to my brothers-in-arms, I tried a different route.

"Tres is family." I held up my hand when Geraint and Gawain went to protest. "And we don't leave family behind."

Gerry closed his eyes and pinched the bridge at his nose. Wain shook his head and looked the other way.

I turned back to Thor. "Anyway, I just want you to know that."

"Know what?" he asked.

"That I'm not using you."

The big bear of a man grinned down at me. "I don't think I'd mind if you did."

I tilted my head and pursed my lips as I took in his narrow hips and powerful thighs. He had big feet and long, thick fingers. If it were literally any other time but this moment ...

"I'm sorry," I said. "But I am going to use your tool."

Thor's grin spread impossibly wider. "I'm certain I won't mind if you—"

I reached down and relieved him of his hammer. His grip was slack around its hilt. He could've yanked it back from me, but he didn't. He could've called it back out of my grasp, but he didn't.

Instead, he lifted a brow and watched me with interest. I twirled the hammer in the air, aiming to get its full impact. The knights grabbed onto the wall sconces, but it didn't help. Everyone lost their footing when the mallet struck the floor leading to the hall doors. Everyone except me and Thor.

While everyone was down, I raced down the hall. I headed for the great door, the entrance to Valhalla.

"Loren," shouted Tres as he scrambled back to his feet. "What are you doing?"

"What my instincts tell me to," I shouted over my shoulder.

Bryn was the first of the Valkyrie to her feet. "Back away from the door, pest."

"No." I put my back to the door with the hammer cocked to my ear, ready to turn and give the jamb a whack. If it could knock these children of God off their feet, it was no match for a thick piece of wood. "We're coming to a new arrangement. I get all my friends back; Nia, Zane, and Tres. In exchange, you get to keep whatever is behind door number one."

I had to assume that the dead behind this door was more trouble than me. So, I figured worst case scenario, I save Tres and something wicked this way comes. The Valkyrie would be too busy to chase us because they'd be fighting the big bad, and we could all escape.

"Thor," said Hilda, "call your hammer back."

"Can't." Thor leaned his big body against the wall. "I'm going to marry that woman. I don't want to start our lives together with an argument about that time I took your side over hers."

The pain was palpable in Hilda's eyes. Unfortunately, that particular expression didn't translate to man-glish. Only a woman could read the expression.

"You know what will happen if she opens those doors," said Hilda.

"So." Thor shrugged. "Give her what she wants. What harm will it bring to you? I doubt your mother would appreciate you holding an Ishim captive while they still have work to do in Midgard."

Work? What work? Tres seemed unaware of his job duties as well by the confused look on his face.

"I've had enough," said Bryn. "I'm done playing tricks with a human pet."

Bryn unsheathed her sword. With a flick of her wrist, it flamed up. The Valkyrie let out a terrible scream as she charged me.

Bryn ran at full speed and she wasn't stopping. Looked like I'd have to go through with my bluff.

I swung the hammer, crashing it into the door.

Bryn backpedaled as the wood splintered. Her face looked stricken, and my bravado slipped. No one moved. No one breathed.

All gazes were wide as they stared at the crack in the door. Slowly the massive door swung open. And all hell broke loose.

20

I'd been inside men's locker rooms before. High school lockers with smelly gym clothes and cloying, cheap cologne. College lockers with moldy, neglected textbooks that were highlighted in Gatorade stains rather than pencil marks. I'd even made my way into a professional sport players' locker room.

Paris, World Cup, 1998. I'd snuck in and snagged a pair of Beckham's underpants. I didn't keep them, that would be gross. I sold them on the black market. Not so much for profit. More for fun. I got a kick out of watching the elderly heiresses start a bidding frenzy to score the jock strap.

Those locker rooms had been clouded in hard-fought sweat, recreational herbs, and disinfecting antiseptic. Walking into the open entryway of Valhalla, I was brought to my knees. It went beyond armpit funk, foot fungus, and sweaty balls. It was the rank smell of a ten thousand-year-old locker room that had never once been cleared or aired out. That was the only way I could describe the burning nose hair of a smell.

By the looks of who was inside, I doubted my locker room analogy was far off. The room was filled with men. Men for as far as the eye could see, and the hall was endless.

There were men of all shapes, sizes, colors, dress, and even undress. The vast sea of men rose and fell like waves. Down in the trough, men lounged. They laid on couches and played games, slumped in chairs as they scratched themselves, and slept on the floor in the fetal position.

Up in the crests, heads bobbed and snapped as fists and feet connected. Lips split and flesh cracked open, but not an ounce of blood spilled. Not even one drop. They had no blood. These were all dead men.

On and on the wave of males rolled. Up in aggression, down in nonchalance. Bodies crashed, and were beached, and then pulled back into the fray.

"What the hell?" I whispered.

"Exactly," said Siggy. Her voice was a strained whisper in my ear. "This is hell. These are the souls of the worst that humanity has to offer."

Gathered in a corner were a number of Asian men with long wispy beards wearing silk with spots of red at their heart. I remembered my father telling me that the Mongol army of Genghis Khan would wear silk beneath their armor so that if an arrow pierced their skin it would be surrounded by the soft material and easier to remove.

In another corner were many dark skinned males with the rounded facial features and tightly-knitted hair of eastern Africa. Many modern-day descendants of the African diaspora had thinner noses and more angled cheekbones due to the inter-mixing of cultures. It was the British-style uniforms these men wore that had me taking a step back. Continental Africans in colonizer's fatigues was never a good sight to behold.

"Khans, dictators, generals, cartel leaders," said Siggy. "Sooner or later they wind up here."

"This is your army?" I asked.

"No," said Hilda. "What would we need of dead men to fight a battle between gods? They power all of Asgard with their egos and testosterone. They are perpetual energy. We keep them so that their souls won't be reborn."

"Now," Siggy wrapped a hand around my forearm, "back away before they see that the door is open. Or worse, they see you."

I took a step back along with Siggy. The floorboards cooperated, not making a single creak. The heel of each of our boots somehow muffled against the hard surface of the floor. We were nearly out of the clear.

And then a glass shattered.

There was a jerk of awareness in the wave of men. My heart plummeted to my stomach. Time slowed down as I tried to determine if I should stay and fight or run in flee. But first, I needed to know where that crash originated from. I turned to see Loki.

"Whoops," said Loki. He leaned against a wall where a statue had once stood. The decorative piece was now in a shattered pile on the floor. Loki didn't look the least bit apologetic. He glanced up at Bryn and winked.

"You dragon's arse," Bryn hissed. She took a menacing step towards the trickster god, but he waggled his finger and pointed past her at the open door.

The men inside the Hall of Valhalla looked up. There was a pregnant pause, a shared breath, and then the air changed.

Siggy and I rushed to bolt the door, but an arm blocked the way. Then another limb. And a leg. The others on our side came and lent their strength. But it was three Valkyrie, three knights, an Ishim, and a god against thousands of angry souls hungry for freedom.

"You idiot," shouted Bryn.

I looked at the space where Loki had stood. He wasn't there. Bryn's gaze wasn't on that spot. She was glaring at me. I was the idiot.

"How was I supposed to know what was behind the door?" I said.

"Oh, you're right." Bryn opened her eyes wide with false innocence. She balled her hands and held them to her heart in fake sincerity. "If only someone told you not to open the door where we stored the dead."

While we were busy arguing, the first man slipped out. He was Asian, short in stature with a large head and small eyes.

"Is that Attila the Hun?" said Tres.

"No," said Geraint. "I think it's Genghis Khan."

"Are you trying to say all Asians look alike," said Gawain.

The Hun or Khan let out a battle cry and charged. Geraint stepped forward and threw a punch, but it went through the man. Hilda lunged in, her sword igniting with firelight. She sliced into the dead warrior's torso.

The dead man's legs raced one way before sinking to his knees. His chest fell the other way. His head crashed down at her feet.

"They're not corporeal," said Hilda. "They're pure energy in the shape of men."

The energy of the dead men pushed back against the crowded door. Siggy and Bryn managed to get one side of the doors to swing in on them. Unfortunately, it wasn't enough force to close the latch which I had broken with Thor's hammer.

Another live corpse escaped through the cracks. This one was black as night and dressed in a green soldier's uniform. I knew this face. He was Idi Amin, the violent Ugandan dictator who massacred nearly a half million souls. The look in his eyes told me he was looking to add more to his previous life's body count. Amin pushed and shoved his way through the door. I wasn't sure how a being who was corporeal could move something solid.

Siggy sent up a piercing cry. As the screech rang up to the rafters, I felt the Valkyrie running towards us. Their pounding boots shook the floor as they filed into the hall.

The doors of Valhalla quaked as men pushed and shoved toward their freedom. A few more filtered out. I saw the familiar mustaches of Lenin, Stalin, Hitler. With all our might we managed to shut and bolt the doors back. The Valkyrie shoved swords and shields into the hole as a makeshift patch.

There were at least two dozen men that had escaped. Siggy and others took off after them. Bryn remained behind with a few of her sisters.

"Millennia of hard work gone because you couldn't take yes for an answer," she said to me. "You are the worst of humankind. I think I'll make an exception and put a woman in the hall of those men."

Bryn drew her sword. Geraint, Gawain, and Tres surrounded me. And then Thor stepped in front of us all.

"She's mine," he said simply. "You want her; you go through me."

Bryn kept coming. She let out an ear-piercing scream. Her entire body glowed bright. The Valkyrie behind her followed suit. They screamed and lit up as well.

We were trapped. There was no way out of this. It was an impossible situation. And then I remembered, I had one more play in my back pocket.

I reached into my back pocket and slipped on the ring just as the Valkyrie charged. Thor let out a mighty roar that shook the rafters of the hall and charged toward them. All of a sudden, the Valkyrie stopped advancing, but it wasn't because of him.

The Valkyrie stood and stared at the spot where they'd last seen me. They lowered their swords as they looked left and right. Thor turned and looked over his shoulder as well. His gaze widening in disbelief.

"What happened?" said Tres, who stood at my back. I felt his heart pounding against my spine.

"Why can't they see us?" asked Gawain, who stood at my right shoulder. "Why can't they hear us?"

I didn't need to explain any of this to Geraint who stood at my left shoulder. He looked down at the ring on my finger. Then he looked back at me. The color and the feeling drained from his face.

21

"Where did they go?" Bryn shouted into my face.

I felt her spittle on my cheek. The spice of the mead she'd drank earlier burned my flesh. Her sisters spread out around us, their swords coming close to Tres's shoulder. He took a step closer to me.

"It's witchcraft," said one of the Valkyrie.

Nope. It was fae magic. From the dining hall doorway, I caught sight of Gyges. He looked directly at me even though his ring made me and my friends invisible to every other eye. His purple lips quirked in a mischievous grin. I had to wonder if he and Loki were somehow related.

"That's it." Bryn's eyes lit up like she finally had the answer to a trivia question that had irked her for days. "That's how she came through the Bifrost alive. That's why she was at Yggdrasil. She's a witch. The men must be wizards. We've been breached."

Hilda tilted her head, as though to shake it in protest. But she stopped before she could complete the motion. She angled her head instead toward Thor.

"You were at Ran and Aegir's when they arrived," Hilda said. "She's just a human caught in one of their nets. Right?"

Thor didn't answer as he looked at the empty space that was where I stood and saw nothing. But by the way his nostrils flared I knew he could smell me.

Hilda stepped in front of me, barely missing my toe. She glared at Thor until he gave her his attention. "Is this true? Is she a witch?"

Thor didn't deny any of it. In fact, he nodded and then reached for her wrist. "Hilda, you are my oldest friend. You know—"

Hilda yanked her hand away. "I know that I've endured your philandering for centuries."

"You've *endured*?" Thor asked. "What do you mean?"

Hilda swallowed, her ire losing a bit of traction. "You've gone too far this time. You've put the safety of all Asgardians in harm's way because you were thinking with your prick."

"I was thinking with my heart," Thor insisted.

Any fight remaining went out of Hilda at those last words.

"She's not here for the tree or its magic," said Thor. "She's trying to find—"

But Hilda turned from him, effectively silencing him. "They can't have gone far. Spread out and find them."

"We need to get those souls back," said another sister.

"All would've been well if we'd have thrown them in the Bifrost when they first arrived," said Bryn.

As the arguing continued, I motioned the guys backward. We walked away in silence, turning a few corners until we came to another doorway. I hesitated to turn the knob, but it couldn't have been worse than what lay inside the Halls of Valhalla.

I held my breath as the door creaked open. There were no foul smells of armpit and jock itch in the air. The room was empty, save for an ornate wooden chair at its center. A massive fireplace decorated one end of the wall. Paintings spanned the other three walls; paintings of young girls with pointy ears and fire in their eyes.

I was guessing they were portraits of each of the Valkyrie sisters. Was this some sort of family room? But why only the one chair?

I slipped the ring off my finger and immediately regretted it. The loss of the ring's cover rendered me vincible, which I knew for a fact was a real word. I felt utterly vinced by the look on Geraint's face, which was devastating. I wouldn't have been surprised if his visage could've smash Thor's hammer.

I opened my mouth. Then closed it. Then opened it again.

"Don't," Geraint said. "There's nothing you can say."

Geraint gave me his back. His shoulder blades were great, bulging rocks of tension. There was no pathway up, around, or through him.

I looked at Gawain. His gaze was locked on my hand where I held the ring over the tip of my index finger. Unlike Geraint, Gawain's features weren't impassable. They were worse. His gaze was clouded with disappointment.

"I ..." My voice croaked and I had to start again. "I wanted to tell you."

"When?" Geraint whipped back around, but he didn't move toward me. He took a step back, increasing the distance between us. "Rome was weeks ago."

"I know." I held up my hands for him to keep his voice down now that we were no longer under the ring's protection. "Gyges slipped it to me."

"Here?" Geraint's brow lowered ever so slightly. Hope was at the corners of his eyes.

It would be so easy to lie. So easy to take that out, that Gyges had slipped me the ring tonight. I hung my head in answer.

Geraint made a harsh sound, likely a curse in Arabic because even Tres winced.

"I didn't realize I had it until we were back home," I said. "Then I didn't know how to tell anyone. I was going to—"

I stopped talking at the sound of Geraint's laughter. I hoped for a second that he'd let me in on the joke. I needed to laugh right now. But his mirth was humorless.

"You fooled me." Geraint's hands dropped to his sides, but the boulders remained at his back. "I let you fool me. Once a thief, always a thief."

"That was way harsh, G." The corners of my eyes stung. I lifted my head to keep any tears at bay.

"Only hurts 'cause it's true."

He met my gaze then. I expected to see a

glimmer of remorse, a spec of regret. There was none. His gaze was hard as granite. The bridge of friendship we'd built over the last few weeks had crumbled. But there was a light at the end of the rainbow.

Rainbow?

There was a rainbow glowing from somewhere in the room.

We all turned to the multicolored light that ignited the dormant fireplace. I felt the unmistakable and welcome energy of a ley line. It wasn't the bright colors of RGBIV, it was more pastel with pinks and limes and teals. When vines grew in the hearth, Geraint let go of his angry visage and rushed to the fireplace just in time for a woman to step out.

"You," said Geraint. But he stopped as soon as she started to move.

Enid held up her hands in warning. She looked weary, her clothing disheveled, her hands crusted with dirt. But veins were visible at her fingertips. Geraint had been at the business end of her thorns before.

"You said you would help if ever I needed it," said Enid. Her voice was low and breathless. Her gaze was haunted.

"Yes," Geraint said. "Yes, whatever you need."

"I am in need." Enid didn't move out of the fireplace. The vines around her feet pulsed, inching closer to Geraint with their thorns gleaming in the pale rainbow light.

Geraint didn't seem to notice. He bowed to her, the boulders that had been at his back when he'd addressed me crumpled. "I'm at your service, my lady."

"Will you come with me?" she asked.

Geraint hesitated. His head turned, but he didn't look over his shoulder. His eyelids lowered instead of lifting to take me in. I watched his chest take in an unsteady breath and then let out a smooth exhale.

He took a step forward. "Lead the way, my lady."

I reached out to him. It was with the hand from which the ring still dangled. It was too late. He took decisive steps away from me until he was beyond my reach.

"I'll go with him," said Gawain.

I opened my mouth to protest this turn of events. That fairy chick didn't tell anyone of us where she was going, what she needed help with, or what dangers they might face. Geraint was already stepping into the prism glow of the fireplace. Gawain was back stepping to join him.

"You go get Nia," Wain said to me. "I'll stick with him. We'll talk about this when we get home."

And then they both were in the fireplace. My two G's surrounded another woman instead of me. My cheeks burned with the effort of keeping my mouth shut and my eyes dry as I lost my brothers.

Enid lifted her gaze to the door of the hall. "They'll be coming soon."

I didn't need to ask who. I knew she meant the Valkyrie.

"This hearth is Odin's access to the Bifrost," she continued. "It works much like a ley line. Once we leave, you can use it to return to your realm."

"Could it get us to Niflheim?" I asked.

Geraint let out a breath and shook his head. I ignored him. I'd lost one, potentially two friends today. The least I could do was try to save another.

Enid shook her head. "Only Odin's hammer can get you into Eden's realm."

I closed my eyes in defeat. So, I was worse off than before. I'd broken the treaty. Nia was still trapped. And now I was losing my brothers. When I opened my eyes, the three of them were gone. The fireplace didn't have an ember glowing, but I felt the energy pulsing from the magic beneath it.

"Loren?"

I'd nearly forgotten that Tres was here. Now I'd have to hear him let me have it, too. I'd ripped Tres's selfless deal with the Valkyrie in tatters. Now neither of us could be the hero.

"We should go," said Tres.

My throat was sore from pleading and begging, but I forced words past my lips. "You're not going to abandon me too?"

"Why would I abandon you? You just saved my eternal soul."

"I still wound up being a villain," I said. "No matter what I do."

"You're my heroine."

Tres reached out his hand. I took it. He was warm and solid. I had the strong desire to curl into his chest and rest for a thousand years. Instead, I walked with him toward the fireplace. The closer I got to it, the stronger the ley energy called to me, but I didn't answer it. Not yet.

"What are we going to do about Nia?" I asked.

"We'll figure something out," Tres said.

I felt bone weary. All this for nothing. We'd failed in our quest, and now I'd have to go home, tail between my legs and face Arthur. I was wondering if it might be a better fate to stay here and let Bryn toss me into Valhalla with thousands of aggressive men.

No. Facing Arthur was marginally a better fate. I reached out my hand and prepared to call the ley line forward. Before my palm could even warm, a great gust of energy exploded from the hearth, knocking both Tres and me back on our asses.

When we looked up, an old man dressed in gray rags with a crumpled hat on his head stepped out of the flame. He tilted up his head and looked at us with one eye; one shining, bright eye that burned more brilliant than the sun.

The pieces of the puzzle fell together. The throne at the center of the room, the pictures of the young Valkyrie that lined the wall, the private doorway. This man, staring down at us like we were tres-passers was Odin, the All-Father.

22

———

The All-Father god stared at us with his one good eye. I kinda got the feeling he could also see us with his bad eye. That one, legend told, he'd offered up for a taste of knowledge. Tres and I stared back at him. The three of us were mute in the long hall until the banging started at the door.

Tres shoved me behind him. But that position didn't put me in a safer place. They Valkyrie were at the door and their father was blocking our ley line exit at the fireplace. There was no escape.

The banging increased, enough to shake the door hinges. Odin turned his monocle gaze from us to the door. His high cheekbones drooped as he let out a loud and weary sigh.

Could it be? The All-Father didn't want to see his

daughters any more than we did? I got my answer a second later.

My heartbeat slowed, like a train breaking as it pulled into the station. My blood ceased its rushing through my veins and instead slogged the last few inches, like a locomotive on the train tracks as it came to a stop. I didn't feel the need to inhale. My eyes stopped blinking. It was as though time had frozen.

Because it had. Odin held up his hand toward the door. When he lowered it, I saw the energy move around him like water, like we were nothing but fish moving through a vast pond. He held us still in a long, drawn out second as he observed us. The light in his single eye twitched like it was scanning us, pulling up a report, and taking a moment to read it.

"Ah," Odin said finally. "Tresor Mohandis. Also known as King Gilgamesh. And many other aliases. Precisely four thousand nine hundred and thirty-two years of age. Son of the Elohim Michael and human woman Amirah, brother of Zayin."

"What?" gasped Tres. We were frozen within a second of time. I didn't think that air wasn't necessary. But he gasped again. "What?"

Odin didn't answer him. The elderly god turned

that calculating eye on me. "Loren Van Alst. Also of many aliases. Exactly twenty-five years—"

"Hey!" I protested him saying my age out loud in front of present company. Even though Tres had many millennia on me, a lady never revealed her age. As far as anyone knew, I'd been twenty-one for a number of years now.

"Daughter of Dr. Victor Van Alst and Magda Galahad."

Tres and I both stared dumbfounded, unmoving, completely shaken.

Odin turned from us and made his way over to the throne. He moved like an old man. The sound of his bones creaking filled the silent second.

As he made his way into the chair, he left the fireplace unblocked. Neither of us took the route to our freedom. We both turned to the god on the throne. It was then that I noted the hammer hanging on the wall beside him.

Tres saw it too. He shook off his shock and narrowed his gaze at me. I knew Tres and I were in agreement as I looked into his eyes.

We'd both been through a great deal these past few weeks on our quest to save Nia and Zane. That mission had always been at the forefront for us if for no one else. And so we turned our back on the fireplace. Before either of us could bring up the hammer or our friend, I asked the most pressing question.

"How did you know all of that about us, about our families?"

"I know everything," said Odin as he arranged himself on his throne. He settled with a sigh as his old bones found the most comfortable position. "Well, most everything that has already happened. Which affords me enough insight to predict the future. I know why you're here."

He reached for the hammer beside the throne. Again, his hands pushed aside waves of energy. I tried to take a step toward him, but it was as though I was moving through molasses. The weight of the energy felt like a ton crushing down on my shoulders, leaving me uncoordinated and sluggish. Tres moved with a bit more ease. The move he made was to take hold of my unruly limbs and bring me to him.

Odin watched us with interest. "Do you know I recently spoke to your father?"

I was certain he was speaking to Tres, since my father was dead. But when I tore my gaze from the hammer and met Odin's single eye, he was looking at me.

"Well, of course, you wouldn't know that," he said. "You have no access to Hel."

"Hell?" My voice croaked. "My father's in hell?"

"Of course," said Odin. "He died."

The only thing holding me up in the thick air was Tres. If I had my way, I'd have collapsed into the floorboards, all the way through the realms to join my father. Because if he was in Hell, then I belonged layers below him.

My father was a good man. He'd never done anything but try to help people. He'd made one mistake in his life, one mistake. It had taken me years to clear his name. But it hadn't helped. He was being eternally punished for it.

"Oh," said Odin. "I forgot what you humans believe of Hel. It's nothing like what is written in the storybooks. It's rather comfortable. So comfortable that many souls decide to stay."

"Wait?" I said. "My father is alive?"

"Alive isn't the right word. Energy never dies. It simply changes form. Anyway, Dr. Van Alst and I were speaking on the matter of daughters and—"

"So my father's form is in the realm of Hel?" I shoved against the oppressive air, trying to get closer so that I wouldn't miss any part of his answer.

Odin pursed his lips. I got the impression he

didn't like being interrupted. I also got the impression that it happened a lot. Made sense if he had a couple dozen rowdy daughters, that he was often away, and when they came banging at his door, rather than opening it, he froze time to get a little peace and quiet.

"He was in Hel," Odin said. "But he decided to be reborn. As I was saying, I asked his advice on raising such a fine daughter. Word has gotten out about you and Dr. Rivers in the nine realms. Do you know what your father said?"

My heart was in my throat. My ears were ringing. My eyes were stinging.

"He said a father should encourage his daughter's assertive nature and play down any differences between males and females."

The corner of my lip quirked up in a grin. That sounded exactly like my father. He never treated me any different because I'd been born a girl. Which was one of the reasons he started my fencing lessons. He'd said he would've done the same with a boy so there was no reason to not do it even though I'd one day grow breasts.

"Fine advice," Odin was saying as I came back to the present. "I do that with my daughters. They're all assertive warriors who would decimate any male. Don't you think?"

Odin addressed this question to Tres. With my back still pressed against Tres's chest, I felt him gulp before he answered.

"They are, indeed, fierce warriors."

Odin seemed pleased at that pronouncement. "Yes. I think I'm on the right track with them."

I remembered the sound of his girls pounding away at the door outside to get inside and likely kill me. He could stay on the homicidal homeschooling track with them if he so chose. I had other matters to attend to.

"Anyway," Odin stood, holding his hammer out towards us. "This is what you came for."

Just like that. The prize we'd all nearly died for. It was being handed to us by an all-powerful god. But I couldn't move through the sloughing energy to grasp it.

Tres took the necessary steps to take hold of the prize. Odin placed the hammer in Tres's outstretched hands. The moment the hammer touched Tres's flesh, time resumed.

The doors shook again. Odin groaned. He came away from the throne with much quicker feet, but he still wobbled. Tres handed me the hammer and offered an arm to Odin. The three of us made our way to the fireplace as the door to the hall was quickly being reduced to kindling.

"Be sure and say hello to their mother for me while you're down there," said Odin. "She should make a point to visit the girls. It's been an entire millennium since she's taken any time off from her work."

I couldn't help myself as the wood of the door splintered. "Maybe you should spend some time with them yourself. I think they might be in desperate need of a firm hand."

Odin only wrinkled his nose at the idea. "Not at this particular time of the century. You know, women's trouble."

Tres wrinkled his nose in the same fashion. Compassion lit his eyes. I was all set to protest men and their aversion to the natural goings on in the female body, but Tres gave me a yank.

A bright flame ignited in the hearth. Odin stepped inside. In the blink of an eye, he was gone. And it wasn't a moment too soon. The second the fire doused, the door burst in.

Valkyrie filled the door, led by Bryn. Her eyes burned bright and wild. She took one look at the hammer in my hand. If possible, the flames burned even wilder. She let out an ear piercing scream and charged.

I grabbed onto Tres. Raising the hammer over my head, I bent down and smashed it into the floor and the world went black.

23

"**Y**ou should take this, too."

After handing Arthur the Ring of Gyges, I now offered him my sword. The sword had belonged to my grandfather, Sir Galahad, the second of his name. My mother had stolen it when she'd run away from Camelot to marry my dad.

She'd been a thief too. Even though the sword was her birthright. But no one called her a thief, not to her face anyway, because she'd run away. Once again, I'd be following in my parents' footsteps.

I'd told Arthur everything. That I'd had the ring since coming back from Rome. That I'd never once considered following his orders to stay and not go after Nia—but he obviously knew that. That I was responsible for breaking the treaty between the realms.

He listened quietly. And by quietly I mean he didn't say any words, but his dark gaze spoke volumes. He looked every bit the imposing dark knight as he sat at his place of honor and leadership at the head of the Round Table.

Of course, the table was round, but the eye immediately drew to him and held. Arthur was the beginning of the line that formed the circle and the end of it. All the spaces in between would not exist without him there.

My glance slipped to my family seat. I stood opposite the seat of Galahad now. I let my gaze caress the comforting cushions of the chair that molded to my back every time I'd sat down in it. I had treasured each time that I had taken my place there like it could be the last. Because I knew the likelihood was real. And now that moment was here.

Arthur had the Ring of Gyges in one hand. He took my sword from me with the other. The connection between my brain and my fingers shorted and my fingers jerked, closing around the hilt, unwilling to give it all up.

But I had to. I had no choice. I let go.

My sword, Inigo, was all I had to turn over to end

my time as a knight. There was no badge when a squire ascended to knighthood. There was a ceremony and dinner. Then you were a knight. They couldn't take the food back.

Without my sword, I felt naked, but I didn't deserve it anymore. I'd put my entire family in danger, left them vulnerable. Again.

I wasn't a knight. I was a nuisance. Arthur was likely glad to be rid of me.

"You think I didn't know you had this?" He held up the ring to the light. It twinkled at him like a coquette. "We live in an enchanted castle. There's a seer in the kitchens as well as a technological genius past the dungeons. Percy detected the ring the moment you came back. Igraine told me you'd get it before you left."

"Why didn't you say anything?" I asked.

"Why didn't you?"

I opened my mouth. Then closed it.

"I can understand why you didn't tell Gawain or Geraint. You're still learning each other. I assumed you'd tell Gwin and Morgan, at least. Those two you trust."

I shifted in my boots, wanting so bad to turn away from his steady gaze. "That's why I'm turning in my resignation. Effective immediately."

"We've had this conversation before, Loren," Arthur said, rising from his seat. "You offered your life in exchange for mine the last time. Remember that?"

Of course, I remembered that. Merlin and the Banduri had laid siege to the castle back then. Then one of the Banduri had laid a blade at Arthur's neck. I was expendable. Camelot couldn't exist without its Arthur.

"Now you offer a ring and a sword." Arthur came to stand before me. Said ring and sword in his hands. He slammed them down on the table. "I want you, Loren."

The ringing of the blade and the clatter of the ring took a moment to go silent in my ears. When the high pitched pulsing stopped, my brain was still spinning. What did he just say? He wanted me?

Crap!

Arthur was in love with me. How did this happen? What was I gonna tell Morgan?

"I want you to stop running," he continued. "To stop hiding. To stop lying. Put your thong or whatever on and grow the hell up."

My mind was reeling from the emotional arsenal he was using to lay into me. First concern, then a guilt trip, a bit of humor, stirred with a heap of anger and frustration. When had he become a master of the emotional argument?

"You don't get to quit." It was a growl that tore through him. But the sound was a low and quiet rumble, which made it feel all the more deadly. "You don't quit on family. You don't quit the table. Those vows are for life. We don't do divorce."

"But I screwed up. I disregarded your orders. I put the whole town in jeopardy. And you're down two knights. All because of me."

"Yeah," Arthur agreed. "Everything I said would happen—imagine that. What is it with you? Is it a sexist thing? Is that the reason you thumb your middle finger at my commands?"

It wasn't a rhetorical question. I knew because he didn't give me a chance to answer.

"I give you chance, after opportunity, after benefit of the doubt. But you still insist on defying me. Is it my hair? Does the cut offend you? Or maybe my fashion sense? I'm too last century? What makes the three of you Galahad girls not listen to me?"

"Your cologne, maybe?" I lifted a shoulder.

"I don't wear any."

"Precisely." My bravado was failing as I rushed on, giving him the full truth. "You exude natural confidence, leadership, and know how. All things women have to fight to prove they have. I keep expecting you to figure out that I don't have a clue as to what I'm doing."

"Oh, I know that," Arthur said. "I have you completely figured out. You're a scared little girl with abandonment issues. The worst kind of abandonment issues because you know what it is like to be loved and cherished. You're terrified of finding and losing that again."

I took a step back from him. But there was nowhere to run.

"You know that love can be taken away and there's nothing you can do about it. Even if you raised a sword or flashed a ring or slammed down a hammer. That's why you fight so hard for those you care about. But when we try to do the same for you, you push us away. Just like those other two Galahad girls."

Arthur ended his grand speech with a sigh and a pinch of the bridge of his nose.

"What are you?" I asked. "A shrink?"

"That's one of my degrees," he said. "I've been alive for a long time."

"I'm sorry."

"That's a start."

"Thank you."

"Better."

I hesitated. Then I ran the two steps to him and wrapped my arms around him. Arthur was so big and broad that my fingers couldn't connect behind his back.

"You're still in big trouble," he said as he rubbed at my back.

"I know," I sniffed.

"There will be consequences for your behavior when you get back."

"Yeah," I sighed.

"I trust you, Loren." Arthur pulled away and looked down at me in all seriousness. "That's not a compliment. I trust that you will countermand my edicts. However, I trust that if I were in danger, you'd come to save me. Me or anyone in this town. I trust that you will follow your instincts before you'll follow my commands. You've been lucky that your instincts have been good thus far. But I do not trust you to tell me the truth. That is not good enough. That has to change."

People don't change. Maybe not. But I could try hard to make better choices.

24

———

*A*fter the dangers lurking within the Great Hall of Asgard, I was sure I'd never want to enter a hallway again. But leaving the Throne Room and entering Tintagel Castle's Great Hall was a world of difference from the halls of the Valkyrie.

An arrow came flying from around the corner. It struck my shin, bounced off my pant leg, and clattered to the floor. I picked up the rubber toy and looked around for the culprit.

The only tricksters in this castle were a mere few feet tall. Their little legs couldn't take them far. Their giggles would slow them before they could get away with any mischief.

"You little rascal." I scooped little Phineas Kay up off the floor.

Amidst his squirms and childish laughter, he managed to wriggle free. He grabbed his arrow and took off with his bow to hunt another willing victim. I smiled after him, my heart light.

Within this hall, I never needed worry over losing my head or forfeiting my soul or having the ground ripped from under me with a—

BOOM!

There was no thought for my own safety as I took off. My instincts kicked in. I drew my sword and raced toward the danger inside my home, this place of safety where my family lay their heads each night.

I felt a charging heat on my back. It drew closer, pounding the ground and eating distance. Arthur. I knew it without turning to look.

The sound of the explosion came from the kitchen. People cleared out of our way as Arthur and I raced down the hall. No one else looked frightened or even concerned. When Arthur and I burst through the kitchen doors, we understood why.

"Morgan."

Arthur didn't shout her name. It was more of a wail of pain, like if little Phineas's arrow had pierced Arthur's heart and Morgan happened by and yanked it out.

Morgan and the children around her were all

covered in white powder. The sounds of their gleeful laughter replaced the resonating blast. The acidic smell of vinegar wafted through the room.

"It's fine," she said when she spied us filling the doorway. "We're all fine. We just got the measurements off."

The children all spoke at once.

"Lady Lo! My lord, you should've seen it."

"The bomb exploded so high."

"Look at the stain it left on the ceiling."

I tilted my head up. Sure enough, a yellowish stain was forming on the high ceilings of the kitchen.

"You were teaching the children how to make a bomb?" asked Arthur.

"Not a bomb," said Morgan. "An exploding lunch bag. It's a very simple experiment using household items."

Arthur could only gape at her. His knuckles were white as they clutched at Excalibur.

"No one's dead," she said. "Everyone has their ten fingers and toes. It was a mistake in the measurements. This was an excellent mathematical lesson for the children."

Arthur's eyes bugged out of his head, the skin around his eyes turned purple. He ground his molars so hard I was certain he'd spit out salt. Instead of saying or doing anything, he sheathed his sword, turned on his heel, and slammed the kitchen door.

I didn't miss Morgan's quick exhale of relief before she turned her attention back to the children. "All right, science lesson is done for the day. Clean up the kitchen so Igraine can prepare dinner."

The kids went into motion. Boys grabbed buckets. Girls raised their hands in rhyming spells. The mess would soon disappear without a trace.

Morgan looped an arm through mine and turned us out of the kitchen. "You're back."

"I'm headed out again."

"Oh, no. Are you going to miss the Science Fair?"

"Not sure. Gotta go to the center of the earth and save my best friend and make my way back without getting captured or killed. But I'll try."

"That'd be swell. Thanks, cuz. Well, let me give you a hug now. I might not be here when you get back."

"What are you talking about?"

Morgan's blue eyes twinkled. She pulled her dark hair over one shoulder, twining it around her fingers, and then came out with it. "I'm doing it. I'm going to university after the Science Fair."

Morgan had been accepted into the science departments of a number of Ivy League and prestigious schools for decades. She'd accepted many offers via distance learning. She'd never enrolled in an on-ground program.

"What did Arthur say?" I asked.

"Luckily, he's been so preoccupied with your antics I doubt he'll notice. Thanks for that."

I doubted he wouldn't notice. Arthur was always aware of Morgan. Just like Lance was always aware of Gwin. Everyone was so guilty about their desires here in Camelot.

Morgan could take care of herself. I knew that. She knew that. The only one with any doubt was Arthur.

I made Morgan promise to keep our social media streaks going as she made her move. I gave her another hug and free reign to take whatever she wanted from my closet for her adventure into the coed, human world.

I didn't bother with a change of clothes for myself. I didn't even stop for a shower or another application of eyeliner. Time was nipping at my heels. Luckily, my ride was waiting for me outside.

Tres stood, leaning against the castle portcullis. The gate was lifted. The sharp teeth of the sliding door held suspended over his head. Tres's face was lifted up toward the moon. His expression was guarded, just like it had been in Asgard before the Valkyrie had taken him away.

The night's wind sailed toward me, sending that spicy scent of him to my nose. It warmed my lower lip where he'd tasted me. It stirred the feelings in my head that I had for him.

He looked so alone standing there. I wanted to surrender my goods to him. I wanted to free his body from the oppressive reign of his tailored clothes. I wanted to wrap my arms around him and hold him tight like I'd done with Phineas. Only, if Tres wriggled, I wouldn't let him go.

The impulse to go to him was so powerful that it nearly set my feet in motion. It was my head that stopped me. Choosing to get involved with Tresor Mohandis was a bad idea. There were many reasons why I was sure. But the only one that mattered was Nia.

Guilt gripped me as I looked at the man who'd nearly given his life for my best friend.

I know he felt my gaze upon him. I could feel the energy change. His awareness was like heat. I braced for impact as he turned to me.

"Hey," he said.

"Hey."

Once again, my cheeks heated. Not with embarrassment. With that telltale sign that meant I wanted something.

Tres's gaze slid over me with that silent, wordless awareness. It was so loud it preceded my steps, arriving at his feet before my body did. The goosebumps danced on my forearms. My heart played hopscotch in my chest. The world around us clicked off like a television set powering off for the night.

But Tres didn't turn the set off. He set it to mute. "He let you go? Or are you sneaking out again?"

Tres meant Arthur.

"It's hoes before bros up here in Camelot," I said.

Tres's laughter rolled over me like waves. The sound pulled me under. I'd been shipwrecked before with this man. I hadn't been scared as the boat tossed and turned. Again, I'd felt safe, content, perfectly happy to stand in Tres's cool gaze while the world burned.

Something clicked into place between us. Something unnameable. It clicked again when Tres took a step back.

"Listen, Loren, about what happened on the ship ..."

I stepped back then, dropping any ideas of locks and safe places.

"Do you mean about that $5,000 bottle of Essencia that went missing from the wine cabinet?" I asked. "Because I know nothing about it.'

"I really like you," Tres said, rattling the key in the lock, hovering his thumb over the mute button. "More than I expected to. That's why there can't be anything between us. I don't think I'm capable of a real relationship."

"And you think I am? The last guy I broke up with had the life sucked out of him by Greek gods."

"I almost had the life sucked out of me tonight by Norse goddesses."

He had me there.

"I've never been monogamous." He continued this one-upmanship of who was the worst potential partner.

"Is that some ancient Sumerian word? Because it doesn't translate into my commitment-phobe dictionary."

Tres laughed again, a low, sultry grumble that made me think of a lion stalking a lioness, biding his time before he charged her and took her from behind. The way Tres's gaze hooded told me he was calculating the distance between us.

"This is a really bad idea," he said.

"Really bad," I agreed. "We should go. To get Nia."

"Nia." He elongated the two syllables of her name, as though he needed the time to process who she was.

Score a point for me. I'd momentarily made an immortal man forget the supposed love of his life.

Tres picked up Odin's hammer and studied it. "So, how do we do this?"

"I just spun it, thought of where I wanted to go, and gave the ground a whack."

"Sounds easy enough." He twirled the handle in his palm.

"You'll want to hold onto me tight," I said. "Wouldn't want to lose me on the way there."

Tres took a step closer to me. I met him halfway. He wrapped an arm around my waist. The moment he pressed me into him—

BOOM!

The ground shook, breaking us apart. That didn't sound like a science experiment gone wrong. It sounded like thunder.

When the dust settled, Thor walked towards us. His red hair was like flames. The look in his eyes was hot enough to melt steel.

"There's my bride," Thor said. He pulled me up,

but not onto my feet. My chest met armor and my feet dangled from the ground as he captured me in his embrace.

"What are you doing here?" I asked.

"Treaty is over. I can come to Midgard now."

As I was trying to process his words, he planted a kiss on my lips. I was so shocked my eyes stayed open and landed on Tres. His expression, somewhat open and kinda inviting a minute ago, was completely closed and totally unreadable now.

Thor let me go. Well, he let my lips go but not my body.

"Listen—" I began.

"I know. You haven't agreed to be my bride. Yet. That's why I'm here to court you."

"Court me?"

"I have every intention of winning your affection, devotion, and love, my lady."

Those words, especially the last ones, should've made my skin itch. But they didn't. I wasn't afraid. I was ... intrigued. I was curious. I was interested.

"You look shocked, my angel," said Thor. "I can't tell if it's because you don't think me worthy or because you don't think yourself worthy?"

"I ..."

Tres had turned away. His feet were poised to

walk in the other direction. His tense jaw hid any sign of emotion. Because it was a bad idea. Relationships. But were they?

Someone wanted me. My instinct was to run from that, to hide, to lie.

I knew what it was to be loved and cherished. Here was an opportunity to have that again, with someone sturdier than a human being.

"Thor? Will you put me down?" I asked.

The thunder god hesitated.

"I promise I won't run. Well, that's not entirely true. I have to go somewhere, but when I get back, maybe we can go out."

Thor set me gently on the ground. The grin on his face cracked so wide I thought I heard lightning split the sky. "You are a mighty warrior, my Sif. I know you will succeed in this battle."

"Um, thanks for the vote of confidence."

"I'll be back on your return."

Thor leaned down to kiss me again. But Tres's throat clearing called Thor up short.

"We should get going, Loren." Tres stepped between me and Thor. With Odin's hammer in one hand, he took me in the other.

"Hold her tight," said Thor. "I don't want her slipping away."

"Yeah," said Tres, pressing my body into his until our heartbeats synched. "Got it."

Tres swung the hammer over our heads. His gaze fastened to mine in concentration on where he wanted to go. Even before the hammer's impact into the earth, I felt a shift in my world.

<hr>

The story is not over!
Don't miss the rescue mission as Loren and Tres
journey to the core of the earth
to rescue Nia and Zane in
Eden's Garden
Book Five of the Nia Rivers Adventures.

ALSO BY INES JOHNSON

Lover of fairytales, folklore, and mythology, Ines Johnson spends her days reimagining the stories of old in a modern world. She writes books where damsels cause the distress, princesses wield swords, and moms save the world.

You can sign up for her mailing list and receive alerts and free reads at http://bit.ly/InesReaders.

The Nia Rivers Adventures

Dragon Bones

Demeter's Tablet

Templar Scrolls

Serpent Mound

Eden's Garden

The Misadventures of Loren

Spear of Destiny

Ring of Gyges

Hammer of God